Sealed in Stone

SEALED IN STONE

TONI MARAINI

TRANSLATED BY A. K. BIERMAN

INTRODUCTION BY ALBERTO MORAVIA

City Lights Books
San Francisco

Cover design: Amy Trachtenberg / Robin Raschke
Book design and typography: Small World Productions
Picture credits: Frontispiece, "Arcades du coté de la Rue de la Ferronnerie contenant la Dance Macabre" [detail]; page 8, "Cimetière des Innocents de Paris en 1552"; and page 12, "Cimetière des Innocents de Paris en 1550" [detail]. Chromolithographies originally published in J.Herbert Hoffbauer's *Paris à travers les Ages,* 1870. Courtesy La Bibliothèque de l'Image, Paris 2001.

Cataloging-in-Publication Data

Maraini, Toni.
   [Murata. English]
   Sealed in stone / Toni Maraini ; translated from the Italian by A.K. Bierman ;
         Introduction by Alberto Moravia.
         p. cm.
   ISBN 0-87286-388-3
   I. Bierman, A .K. (Arthur Kalmer), 1923- .   II. Title.
PQ4873.A6913 M8713 2001
853'.914—dc21   2001042126

CITY LIGHTS BOOKS are edited by Lawrence Ferlinghetti and Nancy J. Peters and published at the City Lights Bookstore, 261 Columbus Avenue, San Francisco CA 94133. Visit our web site: www.citylights.com

I dedicate this translation to my dear Kathleen,
who read every word and improved my poetic license.
—AKB

CONTENTS

THE YEAR 1424

THE SETTING FOR THE NOVEL is the Cemetery and Church of the Holy Innocents (Cimetière and Eglise des Saints-Innocents) in Paris. It was one of the most famous places of French medieval history. Both the church and its cemetery were founded in 1137 and dedicated to the Holy Innocents massacred by Herod the Great. The cemetery was desecrated and destroyed in 1785.

More than two million people were buried in the cemetery during the six centuries of its life. "Life" is an appropriate term for this extraordinary place, because it was not just a cemetery. In the big square surrounded by walls, you could find the charnel houses, preaching pulpits, a large fountain, an octagonal tower, the small stands of the public scribes who would write letters by request (Love letters were the most expensive!), the small shops of the book and print sellers and of the men and women who sold religious images and profane objects, such as dresses, used clothing, precious fabrics, hats, flowers, soap, make-up, and so on.

The four walls were arched galleries where people could promenade, admire the frescoes, and visit the small shops and open charnels. In the middle of the churchyard you could also find stands selling food and drinks.

There were four kinds of burial places. Three of them were private tombs and chapels, a common public grave for those found dead in the streets or in the Seine, and a common public grave for those who didn't have the financial means to buy a private space. It was, therefore, *the* cemetery for the Parisian people, who loved this public meeting place. They would go there to consult fortune-tellers. During the daytime they would promenade, buy and sell, admire the new frescoes, pray, and listen to the preachers. In the evening, they would go to meet a lover, or to find refuge and shelter for the night.

But the night wasn't easy there, as it was populated with thieves, killers, runaways mixing with prostitutes, pilgrims, condemned heretics, smugglers, and spies for the Inquisition. Abandoned children, religious mystics, and beggars also lived there, with the gravediggers, the attendants to the dead, and all sorts of monks and friars.

The fourth kind of burial place was for living people. They were immured, sealed up in small stone cells attached to the church's outer walls. For some this was punishment, for others a choice.

In the documents I consulted to reconstruct this fascinating place, which for me became a metaphor of the world itself, I found mention of a young woman called Alix la Bourgotte. A young novitiate of the Hopital de Saint-Catherine, she renounced the world in 1418, and chose to spend the rest of her life walled up in the Cemetery of the Holy Innocents, communicating with the outside world only through an opening the size of a large brick. She died forty-eight years later, venerated by then as a mystic. On her death, Louis XI commissioned in her honor a statue and a sumptuous stone plaque decorated with four copper lions. She is the heroine of my story.

I placed the action in this extraordinary cemetery as it was at the beginning of 1424, and, more precisely, during the famous staging and premier of *La Danse Macabre* or *Triomphe de la Mort.*

All the details are historically accurate. In the winter of 1423–1424, the English conquered the city of Paris. The Duke of Bedford became the Regent of the city. Tradition says that a man who had come with the English invaders set up a big open-air play in the middle of the churchyard—this play was *La Danse Macabre*.

Actors standing on wooden stages decorated with screens and painted panels performed the spectacle. In spite of the presence of the English invaders who attended the premier of the performance with the Regent, the Duke of Bedford, and his entire noble suite, the success was immense. Every Parisian wanted to see the play. The French Duc de Berry charged one of his painters to reproduce the different scenes and characters—and the poetic rhymes—on the walls of the southern galleries. The frescoes of "La Danse Macabre" were visible on the cemetery walls until 1660. François Villon knew them well.

Toni Maraini, 2001

INTRODUCTION

Alberto Moravia

WE ARE LIVING in an inscrutable age that is obstinately and perversely meaningless. The natural tendency of humanity to seek an invisible, ultimate reality beyond the visible, makeshift one flails in vain against this epoch.

In the face of this enigmatic subversion, we can note that, in literature at least, there are two fundamental attitudes: One is that of the writer who accepts the world's meaninglessness and tries to reproduce it in the rigorously traditional game of writing; the other is that of the writer who seeks precisely the meaningful, which seems to doom us to an unbearable, absurd meaning.

The trouble is that the age is not only meaningless, but also objectively catastrophic, and, therefore, is practically not livable, in a completely new way. Ecclesiastes says, "There is no new thing under the sun," but Ecclesiastes was a Bronze Age peasant and mistaken. Two world wars waged on a planetary scale, the artificial replica of death that man created with the atomic bomb, the terrifying phenomena of mass hedonism, ecological destruction, and many other aspects just as likely to crush some so-called values don't permit us to deceive ourselves: Absurdity could, perhaps, be nothing but the waiting room of eternity. Naturally, it's an eternity devoid of living humanity, a meaningless eternity that comes after a time shorn of meaning.

We've already talked about two categories of writers in the grip of the epoch. We have to put Toni Maraini with her strange and necessary novel, *Sealed in Stone,* among those who seek to grasp the invisible reality behind surface reality. Confronting the catastrophic senselessness of our time, Toni Maraini interrogates the past, looking for analogies there. She asks if what we're living through now might not accidentally be a repetition, and if it is, what means did humanity then use to save itself.

The past that Toni Maraini interrogates in order to get an idea about our future is epitomized by the year in which her story takes place, 1424. She chose for her analogy a somber moment in French history, a moment in which the French people were caught midway between a war just concluded and a war on its way to happening.

In a Paris tormented by hunger, the plague, war, and widespread injustice, a Paris that—like Villon's Paris, although unconscious of its own ills, torn between a bourgeoisie that fears the Apocalypse and the plebians who want it—affects the lives of three emblematic characters trying to interpret the obscure and contradictory signs of the times. They are The Big Turk, a beggar poet; the Lombard, a pilgrim for all pilgrimages—and for none; finally, and mainly, a woman who, in the face of catastrophe, decides to take a road opposite to Joan of Arc's: She chooses to have herself walled into a small cell, alive.

Her hermetic cell, or, better, her tomb, was built within the Cemetery of the Holy Innocents, a gathering place, and, one would like to say, a place where the living dead and the dead cohabit. Enclosed forever in her cell, she manages just the same to make a real, living connection with the external world. Toni Maraini's novel is, basically, a singularly exact and articulated description of this relation.

It's the same relationship that the hermits of Thebes, the stylites atop their columns, and, before them, Christ on the cross had with suffering humanity. It is the same relationship, according to Toni Maraini, that would have to be established between the present, murky, and meaningless world and those precious few who seek to give it meaning. (Remember *The Brothers Karamazov*—"So, you admit there are two men who can move mountains.") *Sealed in Stone* is, then, a symbolic description of our epoch. And it is at the same time a kind of historical novel in which history's two equally inscrutable faces—the real and the ideological—are seen with visionary exactness.

Although trying to interpret the future, Toni Maraini is an authentic narrator who reaches into the past. A lyrical tension runs uninterruptedly under a sure and objective style. She shows us a troubled, miserable Paris in which life with its sordid and bloody intrigues seems to release the saraband of a daily Danse Macabre around the woman sealed in her cell. Death triumphs, but, one would say, as an unconscious and stubborn will to live.

And in fact life—not the city's outside the cell but that interior life "inside" the cell—at the end wins its battle against death. Suddenly, the truth, the essential and supreme relation with the world that Toni Maraini calls the Thing, enlightens the recluse. She lets out a cry that sounds like the answer to the apprehensive questions the Lombard asks. With that cry ringing in his memory, the Lombard, baptized, for the second time, by water from the recluse's pitcher, resumes a pilgrimage that finally has a precise purpose.

For this research one has to act as if there were no books in the world. But in the dark night that separates us from remote antiquity, one truth seems clear and eternal, of which one can have no doubt: *This civilized world is certainly made by men,* and, therefore, men can rediscover—because they have to—the beginnings of civilization *within the modifications of our self-same human mind . . .* which, immersed and buried in the body, is naturally close enough to feel what is happening there; but it must make a great effort and exert itself in order to understand itself, as the corporeal eye that sees all the objects outside of itself yet needs a mirror in order to see itself.

—Giambattista Vico, *The New Science, I, 3, 1*

And therefore they . . . cry and laugh at the same time, have hope and fear, feel torrid and freezing, blow both hot and cold, are always embracing everything and never clasping anything, seeing without eyes, having no ears and hearing, yelping without language, desiring without acting, and living dying . . .

—Tullia D'Aragona, *Neo-Platonic Treatise of 1500*

We're as surrounded now with deceit as we were in the past, whose reflection we call history. Only if we interpret one form of deceit with another, does something worthwhile come of it.
—Hugo von Hofmannsthal

1

THE BIG TURK

YES, I WAS THERE the day they walled her in. It was like a May festival. Many people came. Some played music; others threw flowers. There were also those who came to insult her.

You have to understand them. One stayed prostrate for some hours in a corner praying in an unknown language. It wasn't Turkish, I know that. That's so, even if I, who am called The Turk, am not really Turkish. I was born at Famagosta. My father was from Genova and he sailed up and down in the galley that went from Genova to Caffa. The galleys were quick, light as a feather, not like the crocks that are on the seas now, huge, heavy, and as big-bellied as their captains. No.

My father sailed because he had salt in his veins. He distinguished the strong wind and the southwest wind, the sirocco and the north wind, and felt the eastern current from afar. He tested the air and knew which wind ran after the other, watched the water and knew the moon, looked at the moon and found the stars. Then he watched the stars and knew in what direction to go. Yes, he was like the sea, on the move, always ready and always alert. Maybe you could say he belonged to the air more than to the sea, because when he smelled the air he knew the will of the sky that commands the water. He was a sailor in love with a Turkish woman.

And here I am, tied to a dead sea, a troubled land without stars. Alarms rise from below, from some subterranean signal.

Damn! Worthless ship's boy nailed to a boat with an obstinate compass: drawn forward toward the dead. I'm nailed down, under the spell of a sky without winds, without air, without ports. Only one huge port of call. The land is cursed, always there to reduce everything to shreds. Stinking land. My father hated it; he said land is a fraud. For him the sea was a garden, terrible, angry, but always with some smooth corridor somewhere that leads you and carries you away, beyond, toward new ports.

Me? I feel smothered here in this cemetery. This is a citadel within the city, a place where pilgrims and whores, the rich and the poor mingle at endless sermons, feasts, and burials. There's a church in here, rich tombs, and common graves for people like me. Under the arcades are charnel houses, where they deposit corpses and bones. The inner square is a sacred space where we vagabonds and beggars can find protection in the name of Almighty compassion—but you have to pay a token fee to exist here. Christ, yes, here I feel just like a leafless tree in the ground.

After three days docked in port, my father could think only of leaving again. Instead, I travel from one wall to another, from one arcade to the next, under all these scrubbed charnel houses. Ridiculous! A sailor would never have such an idea. Polishing the bones of the dead and lining them up over there, drying them in sight of everybody. How could a sailor imagine such a thing! No, these are things for city dwellers on this side of the Alps, things for sacristans. To put tibias in order and count them!

So here I am, my friend, a vagabond on soil that only the dead plow. Even while you are alive it traps you, invades and conquers you. The stenches conspire, the devils wait, and the dead rush headlong.

The gravediggers are still worse, believe me! What is becoming of me in this port of call? I run from here to there like a hunted fox, counting the money made on lucky days. Tell me. Tell me, where is my garden? That far horizon like a blue line? That calm corridor between the winds? But no, only one wind comes here, from afar, the cold, dry wind that sweeps down from the eastern Alps. It blows between the church and the cemetery entrance like a great frozen tide that rivets you there, stone hard, almost as hard as a skull. It's the only thing that clears out the stench that surrounds all the pilgrims, the curious, those dying of hunger, and even the whores. The cold can do everything!

I was here that very day, before the dawn, when the cold was fierce. The sky was still purple, as if it had forgotten to light up or to black out; it stayed undecided, between the two faces of the coin. It was a sky made expressly for her; I tell you what I've always thought—the weather suits itself to the things of this world. My God, from down here to up there, and from up there down to here there must be an umbilical cord. Whenever we sin, the hail comes, and whenever the moon is late it's because there's a plague.

The sky was purple that day, and that was because it refused to recognize the sun and the moon. It was a sky just for her. In a word, it just was. Then two masons came, escorted by a guard of the parish priest and accompanied by a sacristan half hidden by his cowl. They began to work, mixing soil, lime, and clay. They worked like this for a long time, almost the whole morning in order to finish the three walls attached to the church. Three little, low walls, really a tiny room.

In the cold air their breath was like smoke. And I thought, what if they were a couple of devils in disguise? There was also a funeral taking place under the arcade, but I and my group of mendicants stayed close to the workers to watch; we waited for the spectacle. Maybe today something more unusual than death would happen, we thought. After all, we hadn't made any agreement to see just masses and funerals.

Old Painted-Eyes was there, his toothless mouth gaping open out of curiosity; you could catch a glimpse of his shorn, black tongue that looked like the head of hidden snake. Damn, he was a strange sight. Old and decrepit as he was, he still had thick, bushy black eyebrows, which is why everybody called him Painted-Eyes. No, my Lombard friend, you don't know him; he's not here any more. Do you think that as soon as you get here you know everything? He was from another gang.

Painted-Eyes was an odd sight, hiding himself behind the bushes and watching everything, even the dogs. Where might he be? He died some time ago, weeks or years, what difference does it make? Maybe trapped between hell and purgatory. Will it be like it is on earth there? What could be there for someone like him? Watching, just watching for things, in life and in death. And so like I told you, we stuck around there. Every stroke of the men's spatulas and spades seemed interesting to us while they were building that cell.

We watched, and a little after noon we heard a drum beat. They came right up here, right next to the fountain. A nun, a juror, a prioress, and some guards were escorting an old, closed cart pulled by a mule. Some people hung around to see what was happening, but not yet many because of the cold. The crowd came later, in the evening. I was here too. Right here. The judge read something; I don't know what—no one heard him. We heard the drum roll. But when he approached the cart, for damn sure we all gave him our full attention! It was an old cart, and it seemed like something forsaken, closed and silent as it was. The juror put his hand on the door, opened it, and a young figure, bending forward, came out. I mean a young woman. She came out with tiny steps, blinded by the light. Maybe it was still dark when she'd set out.

She wore her hair cut short, a long dress without a belt, and a cloak. She came forward very, very slowly, and, yes, by God, I liked her immediately. She seemed to me like something to take from between your hands, like the Host. Oh God, I'm certainly an unfaithful, damned soul, but, if I go to church to ask for alms, when I see the Host it moves me. She was pale, light, like no one you ever see around here. Although—fart of a devil—I knew she was made of blood, flesh, life. Jesus, she was a secret world. And she ended up in the guts of this rotten plot of earth. Why else were they hanging around, those devils, so satisfied? As if they'd come to anchor a free spirit, like they did my father's ship he'd navigated by smelling the signs in the air. It was a ship too light for this damned earth, so they loaded it with ballast to anchor it, like her and me in this everlasting dockyard. If not, tell me why they were in such a hurry? One handful of mortar and stone after another, they sealed her in that cell, leaving only a small fissure about the size of a brick.

Shortly before, the prioress had given her a crucifix, but to me it seemed as if the dear creature was unaffected. To tell you the truth, it seemed to me she couldn't care less. To give a talisman to *her*, what an idea! It wouldn't have occurred to me. I would have sung to her, danced a poem, I would have taken her by the hand and had her make a dash for it. I would have given her a bunch of flowers.

She was far away, but they were rooted there. She looked down, and was entirely unmoved. Absolutely serene. Christ, they could have put all the world's ballast here. No other person sealed in a cell was ever so serene.

Then, at a certain point, I trembled, because she looked at me. I tell you, she saw *me*. No, I knew I had never been seen before, I swear to you by all the Holiest Saints, at least not since I've been here, or since my father left me with Genovese traders who came to these lands. The last time I was seen as a person of flesh and blood, five-feet-nine and son of a Turkish woman, is when my father gave me a sack, a few odds and ends, a sealed document, and said goodbye to me.

At that moment she and I saw each other, understood each other, acknowledged each other, each heading toward our own port, a long thread between us that grew steadily stronger.

From then on I was somebody, from the day that she saw me. Yes, she looked at me like someone she knew and recognized in an instant, as one who was lost and found again on the spot. It was a lightning flash, a quick thing. A spark. I was in the first row. Big as I am, with all the things that I've seen in my life, I was rooted there, open-eyed. I saw her, too.

Maybe you can understand me; I've never told anyone. Why? These around here, can they understand me? Perhaps Joshua understood. He knew why I came so often to stand beside the cell to talk to her, and leave her garlands of flowers on the first of May.

To put it bluntly, I was stunned when she looked at me. She cast her eye on everything, you know, the way the beacon on the Genova lighthouse does—a turn, a bright flash, and gone. Then she vanished into that cursed tomb, a young woman. Who knows how it ever happened?

Christ, because I see harlots, bigots, abbesses, and ladies with lice-filled hair, I had forgotten what a woman is, what a fine woman is. An image you put in your heart, to keep with you: You talk to her and she comes every now and then in a dream to rescue you from a nightmare.

Good lord! But what am I telling you, my friend. A raving wretch like me. I'm a half-assed bastard. A complete orphan, that's what—of my country, of the sea, of my mother, dead who knows where or how, and an orphan of my father at the bottom of some sea. I've had enough of this life. Every once in a while this rage seizes me like a tempest, so that I want to put everything to the torch. Yes, it's like a crushing weight on my chest. I can't get my breath and I think of my people, of certain odors.

Once I had a refined nose, because on the Genovese ships there were always spices and perfumed fabrics. There were plants, dried plants, incense, gusts of wind, and fragrances. In recalling them I speak in high style, damn right! In Famagosta's customs house there were cargoes of jars and sacks containing powders, ground leaves, herbs, barks, nuts, essences.

When I was young, I traveled seated on stacks of baskets. I traveled with these odors. I traveled, you can say, with my nose.

Not like these ignorant barbarians, people who feed on cabbage and lard, and who know nothing.

Look, look in this little sack. It looks like a tattered rag. Ah, no, inside there's a little salt. Very, very little salt. Salt. Sea salt, of course. Now with the war it costs almost as much as flour. I keep it here, hidden under my shirt, and every once in a while put a finger in it and taste it. I put a little salt on the tongue and to hell with the gravedigger.

Some have licorice, some relics; others have nightshade or get drunk.

I have magic dust, a little, crude, unbleached salt in big wet pieces. And I have my verses.

Adam of Arras was he perhaps not a hunchback? The lunatics, wandering scholars, the fools—all poetasters and mendicants. I'm not a rogue; I don't tell lies to people and I'm also not a charlatan who amuses people who pass by in order to pick their pockets. First, I amuse myself. Seated, standing, singing or dancing, I do for myself. Without verses I wouldn't live, I wouldn't know how to forget. I would lose my mind.

If people want to listen and I want to give them something, well then, so much the better. Listen to this:

> I'm a wanderer condemned to land.
> Rowing, I row a sea of sand
> always in danger, always begging.
> I'm missing a foot and have no rigging.
> Just empty pockets, not even a coat,
> a powerful oarsman without a boat.
> Fate's delivered me, both hands bound,
> to row this holiest burial ground.

Well, Lombard, my friend, I see that finally you're laughing a little. Oh, you want me to go on? What more can I tell you than I did yesterday after we were attacked by the Gascon and his gang? That Gascon lives out of bounds, a common scoundrel, a rogue, the devil himself. It's because of types like him that I'm here—and who knows how many more of us—damn. Unjustly condemned for robbery, I came to this cemetery for refuge. In fact, someone else was the robber and he shared the loot with cronies, had them testify against me, and I was condemned. Such a simple thing! To tell you how, where, when, would be a long story, a story that's not important any more. I managed to escape the guards, flee at night toward the cemetery. Better the stink of the beggars than to be thrown down, chained at the bottom of a cell filled with water to die rotting and forgotten. I knew no one would ever have gotten me out of there, and every hair on my head stood straight up from fear. That's why, God damn it, I'm here now and here's where I'll stay.

Without a permit you can't live. I can't even work at the market. I'm trapped, like I told you. Who would give me work now—tattered, lame, and patched as I am. At least here they let me be. This cemetery is an asylum for all the refugees. The sacristan protects me because I did my songs for him during the long Passion.

And then I know how to calculate and the others never did. They come to me to ask how much this plus this makes and so forth. I learned to reckon with the merchants. The first one I worked with, a Genovese, really liked me. I was big and strong and was quick in moving the loads of goods in the companies. My father entrusted me to him. They sometimes met along the

Ripa dei Coltellierei: one loaded and the other unloaded. That's how I got to Tortosa, Almeria, and the Brabante. Then one day the brigands took us—that's a long story, too. I ended up with another merchant, but he died. Because I didn't want to enlist with a band of mercenaries, they cut off one of my feet.

And so the vacation ended! Hell, isn't this entire country to be cut off like a foot now? You could say this country no longer exists.

Look, see there? For two days they've been getting ready. And do you know what for? The day after tomorrow there'll be a big spectacle here. Here, right here, in the holiest Cemetery of the Holy Innocents of the city of Paris. The king of the English will come in person. Isn't he the victor? He is. And he'll sit down there, with all the nobility. We'll stay up here, where it stinks more and we'll watch a Mystery play. A step, a pirouette, and here's the King—and everyone is in the presence of death. It's an idea of a great master. Who he is, who he's not, no one knows. He came with the English. He took a place in the preachers' pavilion next to the wooden stand, and directed the action from there. He had a tent and some barracks put up. Don't you see them? What confusion we've seen these last few days?

He's not alone on this trip. His company is here with him. They say he comes from the south, from Provence. They call him Macabré, and he's nicknamed The Moor. A Moor from Andalusia. The spectacle is one of his ideas. And what a spectacle! Christ, the whole city is talking about it. The curious come here and ask, "When? When will it be?" That's why there are so many people around. These actors came up here, up to this powerful ground, and in nine days they'll disinter a body from where the whole city wants to be buried and dangle its skeleton in order to remind us of what we are.

The musicians have already practiced under that tent down there, and the painters are readying the manikins, but to tell the truth, we're not part of the show. Why are we alive? We can give nothing to Death, only some stinking skin and some four-letter words and the crowd will lynch us immediately afterward, because these ignorant people, dying of hunger, always want something more, always something better. In order to forget their troubles, they always want to see more extravagant things, magnificent and astonishing spectacles, and the Moor Macabré is preparing a festival for them such as they've never seen. First, they'll put up a large painting, a landscape of fields and palaces. Then two horned devils with cows' tails and bells will show the crowd a written program.

Well, to tell you the truth, I no longer remember everything, but somebody told me yesterday that's how the show will begin. Then there'll be an actor who will play Death, followed by the Moor Macabré who'll play the Fool, and an announcer who'll call the dead and the living and make them speak.

But why are you looking at me, Lombard, staring like that? Everything I'm telling you is true, damn right. You say you come from Savoy beyond the mountain pass? But what are you doing traveling around the world? In these times, a young lordship like you will be trapped immediately. You won't exist for long.

Don't worry, I'm not an informer. But be careful. Forget what anyone tells you. Here everybody mixes together, all kinds— commissioners of the Inquisition, spies from the ecclesiastical tribunals, heretics and rebels, everybody.

But, getting back to the spectacle, let me tell you one more thing. The best will be like the splendid angel that descended from the castle turret to crown Princess Isabella on the day of her triumphant arrival, a mechanical angel that came down in order to give her a crown. A scarecrow will lift it off. And so everything will be at stake, trembling and repentant, so to speak. They only want to be amused. *Macabar, macabar, tierra de todos, baile de muertos*. Graveyard, graveyard, everyone's fate, dance of the dead. I can still understand the words, because I was in Castile when I was young. But *when* was I young? That's what I'd ask if I got up on the stage.

The Big Turk laughs heartily, slaps his thigh over and over. He laughs at length, closing his eyes and falling back. Then he slowly puts back his tattered sack, refolds it under his shirt of coarse cloth, and gets up.

2

ALIX'S FIRST SOLILOQUY

I KNOW THESE VERSES. I repeated them every day, always expecting that something might happen to end my waiting.

I already felt enclosed in a wall when I ran through the fields where they were burning bundles of wheat and I suddenly saw in front of me towers of very fine, transparent dust. Every thing was itself and also a symbol of something else, as if it had a double life, existed in the cleft of a metaphor.

Then I stopped and everything became lucid. That moment was crystallized, yet liquid. It was resonant. I heard the violent hissing of the magic power that holds everything together: The sun, the surrounding fields, every detail and pebble issued from me, yet they themselves contained me in a space round as a crystal alembic. In that instant, all our assembled throbbings beat as one: my body, the leaves, the stones, the clouds. All the rest was death, the most terrible and total death, when I was not, and rot prevailed.

I would stay like this, absorbed in my vision, until someone called me. Then an invisible net would fall over me again. Once more I felt like a prisoner, as here, now, even though there wasn't this wall that surrounds me in this stifling space.

Without knowing how to get out of such depressions, I would remain for days and hours, waiting, in the grip of a powerful disquiet. I had confused visions of things and details of past events from my life and from lives unknown to me. Facts overlapped; facts rose up in this way, without order, like bubbles of air and mud from the depths of a felt chaos.

Between exaltation and prostration years pass by. I was possessed by something, as if there existed in me a secret cataract, a cyclical sea that unexpectedly flooded all my body's fibers. But I wasn't ready to understand it. Yes, those years passed this way, from the end of my childhood until a little before my father's death. To talk about them now, seems to me like catching them by surprise from another life, rubbed smooth by time.

My behavior was unusual. I was still very young and my family explained my silences and sudden depressions as passing events—a way of growing, that's all. But it wasn't true, and now I know that it was something else. Because we neither grow up nor grow down; rather, we sometimes expand like hot air, and at other times we contract like ice.

At that time the Thing traveled within me. Coming from afar, it shook me, sent arcane messages. I accommodated this tempest but didn't know where to begin to make order within myself.

Yes, my father was puzzled. I was very studious and my idiosyncrasies seemed to him a mark of originality, the proof of a special character. As he had not had male children, and as I was the only child, he was indulgent. Better a daughter who could help him, even if only by bookkeeping, than to suffer her as a deadly burden. The fact is that he had always made me study, and he often took me around with him. From childhood on I had a tutor, a Benedictine monk. The tutor also thought that studying was important for me, but for the opposite reason: To calculate, to pray, to recite entire passages from memory would help me master and control my rebellious, fickle, and original character.

So, I learned to pretend. I acquired the habit of a certain hypocrisy: to hide the vast, troubled space, a land full of horizons waiting to be explored. I learned to follow correctly the rhythm and the phases of daily life. In order to protect this equilibrium—so difficult to maintain—I assumed different ways of being, splitting myself. I was pliant. Yet, within myself I fortified a secret zone, a horizon of which I alone wanted to be the witness. And as in dreams, I fled, faced eclipses and tidal waves. My outward behavior didn't correspond to my hidden life.

It seemed to me that everything I saw, heard, and learned isolated me—each thing in its own way—more and more. I was a witness, but also a powerless body that at the first mutiny would have been annihilated. Yes, I already knew that one day or another I would revolt. But how? Whenever I decided to act, I felt paralyzed and saw the meager shadow of things, exactly, as if, right here in the midst of the spectacle they're preparing here in the cemetery's open space, they were to tear down the columns holding up the papier mâché god and rip away all the masks.

It was thus that I decided one day to look for someone—or something—that finally might help me understand better all that I felt; who might explain to me why I always felt as if I were suspended in mid-air—never among things—yet intensely *inside*, enveloped in the epicenter, that is, at the point where one is invisibly participating, aching. I was looking for someone who might explain to me why I happened to cling to life and at the same time wanted to flee from it with the same passion and the same tenacity.

As the only daughter of a merchant who supplied manuscripts to the university and the episcopal schools of the city, I had to learn to read and write. I had Latin and arithmetic lessons. In my father's house I had always seen many books. Some were ornate, but most had scripted pages with some white panels, which were current books that the purchaser could illustrate himself or have painted by an artist. Other books were embellished by drawings in black and white done in a series, and woodprints in the space left on purpose by the copyist. I saw some books that came from beyond the mountains and from Lombardy with some very thin, white pages. They were quite precious. I liked to look at, touch, and smell these books. I also saw extremely rare ones—my father had bought them after long negotiations—some with painted scenes, precise and luminous, and others that came from distant countries. One from Bohemia had curious pages illustrated by a series of philosophic drawings; another was brought back by a pilgrim to the Holy Land.

These books were for me the world. Just by holding them in my hands, it seemed as if I had read them. They allowed me to imagine. There was one that often was bought by the professors at the university and was produced in collaboration with different copyists. The third page was illustrated by a series of pictures with some portraits—from top to bottom and side-by-side—of Plato, Aristotle, Averroës, Hippocrates, Galen, Avicenna, and Razi. Dignified and serious, they stood in deep thought. Looking at them, I could escape, rove, reflect.

However, my first tutor always complained about my curiosity. He was an old monk and averse to the ancient philosophers, "those heretics." He told me that when he went on a pilgrimage to St. Peter's tomb over the mountains he had stopped in the city of Pisa and there he had seen an immense painting that showed Averroës lost in the human crowd, protesting vainly against the Grim Reaper who, without pity, cruelly rode him down. To him, this was an admonition.

But what he told me in order to discredit the ancients only made me more curious. The concepts he examined, with his prolix and boring reasoning to show me how mistaken they were, acquired instead, in my eyes, a deep power. I thus glimpsed a dizzying dimension of the human spirit. Finally his lessons became unbearable. I preferred to go with my father on his visits to the booksellers' stalls, or to observe some of their business meetings. At times we tarried in the cloister of the Carmelites with some acquaintances or students we met on the way. Yes, we even came this far, along the wall of the church of Saint-Jacques-la-Boucherie, in order to visit the crowded booths of the copyists and second-hand dealers.

My first tutor died, leaving a decent fortune to his adopted son, who was a student in one of his diocese's schools. Then I had a new teacher, a Franciscan friar. The decision was controversial, but my father wanted it thus. A practical man, troubled by the town's events, which were ever more confused and agitated, my father sympathized with the preachers' and reformers' ideas. I had a renewed interest in studying and I read all the time, staying up until late with a lighted candle in a corner, when the bell for the last offices sounded. The lessons were different, for my new tutor didn't bother with philosophy and lost no time commenting on the texts. He talked passionately; current events were his preferred text. He criticized the townspeople, court rivalries, and the defeats in war. In a certain sense, with him I began to glimpse my fears in relation to the reality that I didn't want to accept. It was this reality that I needed to know better.

Then one day I went to the execution of a madman, where also an old witch was being burned at the stake. She shrieked, and at the moment when the stake to which she was tied fell into the pile of burning wood, a terrible grimace contorted her face. The people shouted, furious, accusing her of things I can no longer recall.

The effect on me was so strong that I could no longer listen to what people were saying about other executions. During the insurrection in which my father was killed, I lived as a complete recluse in order not to see the dead with their insides hanging out, without hands, without feet, piled up near the large markets and already being eyed by packs of silent dogs. Putrid smells were everywhere, permeating everything. And unruly people continued to comb the city with the king's soldiers in search of other citizens, other artisans, entire families enrolled under the wrong banner, in search of other bodies to run through with pike and sword.

But I did go out to get my father's body. I went out for I don't know how long. It was dawn. I crossed the bridge up to the square of the market stalls, following the cowled friars who collected the bodies for burial in the cemetery's common ditch. Some of the dead were already stiff and black after having been exposed for two days and two nights on the king's orders. That morning many people were coming and going, wailing, searching like I was.

And although I was seized by horror and revulsion, at the same time I experienced a very strange feeling: I was far removed, unconnected. I had glimpsed something dreadful that violated reality and made it unbearable; an unreal aspect was revealed to me. Nothing could be truer: Life was a conspiracy of apparitions and destructive forces. Only an instantaneous flicker of light made them transparent and transitory.

An unexpected light was pulsing within me like an impalpable wave. But if it was there, I thought, why so many trials, why so much grief? I needed to find an answer that would enable me to understand these facts and these events.

Completely without resources after my father's death, in the confused struggle that divided the city, my mother and I went to live in a residence in the parish of Saint-Eustache. For us, it was a wholly new part of the city. We had always lived across the bridges and the river, at the end of town, behind the college quarters. A painter, who had been an acquaintance of my father, had found us a refuge in this part of the city, in an area where designers and illustrators of manuscripts have little studios and shops.

In the Saint-Eustache parish, the streets are narrow, and full of refuse. The houses, except the court's castle and palace, have no gardens; however, I immediately liked it just the same. The fields began beyond the walls and we could see the distant mills toward the hill. But we weren't used to the vast confusion of that area of markets and butcher shops, always full of people and spectacles. We weren't used to the throng that surrounded the scaffolding to see the swindlers and counterfeiters exposed there, or to the taverns so different from those in the city where the students gathered, nor to the continuous pacing of the merchants up and down Rue des Lombards toward the Pont au Changes.

Nor were we used to the gibbet or the gallows. Walking toward the Marché de la Laine, hanging bodies are always clearly visible. At times there are a good dozen of them. It's impossible not to see them, impossible to pretend not to look. After all, the enormous jail was erected there on purpose so that it could be seen even from the markets. At that time, the gallows of Montfaucon was still there, right in front of us, and we had to get used to it. In the rain, under sun, the bodies dangled in the wind like the teeth of an old man, black and stiff among the flocks of carrion crows.

Indeed, it was another kind of life. Not only had I lost everything, but I had also begun to see beyond my own consciousness, beyond the confused agitation that had gripped me for so long. And I considered this change very important. It was time to face reality and, as they say, to scratch where it itches. In the college quarter where I had lived, life seemed cushioned by velvet, with an artificial veil always thrown over things. Students and professors probably still discuss whether a thing that exists exists, and whether a thing that doesn't exist exists. Probably. So much rhetoric, considering all the important things there would be to talk about, was as insubstantial as dark soap bubbles unable to reflect their iridescence in the sunlight.

Then, at Saint-Eustache, I saw things as they were: The city, life itself, divided in two, perhaps the entire world, the soul. I don't know. This seething place became my daily life. Here the king, the grand duke, the popes, the bishops, and the reformers by turns lose and conquer the souls of the people. They inflame them, deceive them, console them. And, without their knowing, they spy on them, sending agents and inquisitors among them. It was a population that one could never imagine in time of peace; at least, so I think, because when I was born the country was already at war.

But my father's death, the misery, and this new pact with reality were needed to put me in touch with the world's labyrinth. When I went to live in Saint-Eustache, my fears and worries took a tangible and concrete form. I was no longer subject to my own uncertainties, with the risk of paralyzing myself while looking for an answer, but began to reflect on the actual unfolding of both inner and outer reality. I asked myself: Is the world necessarily this way, or does it need remaking? To be changed entirely. And if so, how? Where to begin? I needed to find an answer.

Then it happened one day that my mother asked me to go for her to a notary on the other side of the river, beyond the island and the cathedral, toward where we lived once, in the college quarter. I woke up very early that day; we were just at the beginning of spring—the 9:00 AM bell had not yet rung. I went through the markets, walking beyond the cemetery wall, along the line of scriveners' desks, and arrived in front of the Castle and the prison walls. A new bridge is there now, but at that time you paid a toll to get to the other side.

The sky was crystal clear; the plants in the vegetable gardens and uncultivated grounds were green, luminous, timeless. But the people were in a state of dread. The streets stunk of urine, dogs, and beggars; and Saint-Antoine's pigs were foraging behind the refectory looking for garbage. The people had been here since dawn, wandering back and forth, but I was acquainted with the habits of this street and knew that so much coming and going was not a good sign. It meant hard times.

Back and forth for a permit, forward and backward to get paid, to consult a juryman, to load merchandise, to get an answer from an important person, or simply to look for work. The people were anxious: Whom to trust? In whom to believe? Everybody ended up charging fees and enforcing rules.

The pretext was always the same. One had to wear the green cowl with the Saint-André cross, had to wear the red insignia, wear the violet doublet with the white cross of the king's party, wear the white scarf, wear the marks of the heretic, the lascivious, the sorcerer, the slanderer.

Then there was the contradictory news about battles, truces, and defeats in the great war. Seven thousand dead, a hundred thousand, what difference does it make now? The princesses married just the same, kings signed treaties and organized tourneys; but the insistent rumors ran—the English are close, are advancing, and soon would be at the city gates. Anxiety and distress were perpetual.

I walked along thinking of all these things and then there I was at the little bridge. Before me on the other side lay Rue Saint-Jacques de la Colline, narrow, lively, full of movement. In that part of the city, the houses are taller, more ornate, their facades well kept. You can see all the bell towers, the portals and towers with the insignias of the episcopal colleges, and the university. The Carmelite church was still there, magnificent and beautiful. It seemed to me a century since I'd seen it, although only a few months had passed—maybe a few more—but certainly no more than a year since my father had died and we'd moved to the other side of the river.

That day I had gone to find a notary who had been a friend of my father's, and who took care of his business affairs. He still had some documents and some of our money on deposit. Walking along Rue Saint-Jacques de la Colline, I felt completely alien, so foreign to things that I had to make an effort in order to walk straight ahead and to dodge the passing carriages and their uniformed footmen.

All the people were well dressed. They showed off velvets and furs, walked confidently. At least so it seemed to me. Their cloaks were embroidered. The rectors and the abbots passed with their entourages, the students traveled in groups. Some had to walk slowly because of their long pointed shoes.

There I was, suspended in mid-air. Was it possible we breathed the same air? Occupied the same space? It was as if everything was irrelevant, as if dust had rendered bodies lusterless and images illusory, and that the people, unaware, continued to pretend, pretend to know, pretend to breathe.

Women with tight girdles and colored veils passed by. Back then I would have wanted to hide myself. My cloak was worn and, having no hat, I wrapped a veil around my head. But I was young! After all, once I loved beautiful things, and liked to be elegant. When my father was still alive, during calm times I went around with him and liked knowing and feeling I was young. His acquaintances and friends, and the students, looked at me with respect. I took part in discussions, knew how to recite verses, and also knew some sonnets of the goliards and commentaries on ancient texts. Who knows? Maybe I thought I would be another Heloise. I lived in illusions, and deceived others. But things went differently. The air lightened little by little and concentric currents circled my head, making me forget my hands, feet, everything that was no longer essential to me.

In Saint-Eustache, I often found myself in ragged clothes, but it wasn't important to me. Well, to tell the truth, it was important to me—I didn't want to be noticed because I was too clean or too dirty. I only wanted to be left in peace, and this was possible in Saint-Eustache, where they didn't think of me as an itinerant second-hand dealer—nor as a lady—perhaps just the studious daughter of an artisan, and so I went undisturbed. But now, after months of being away from our former lodgings, I felt completely foreign; my cloak was too long, the girdle out of style, the embroidery faded. I pulled my hair back without ribbons and chignon. No, I was not a lady of rank. No one greeted me or raised his hat, but I walked so straight that people moved out of my way, attentive.

Strange to tell these facts now. Time is strange. It stores facts in the memory like an old invoice. Perhaps the detailed entries are no longer exact, no longer what they were, but the sums, yes, they condense sensations. Dug up again, the invoice returns.

Here, near the Collège de Narbonne I ran into an old cousin of my father's, a rich and stupid courtesan who had managed to salvage her businesses from all the war's perils. I saw her getting off a donkey as she was about to mount the steps that led to the entrance of the college's main portal. I wondered what she could be doing here. Maybe she was coming to influence someone or to bring a gift to the rector. She was painted and dressed-up like an actress in the garb of an old pagan; veils covered her shriveled body. She supported herself with a silver cane and was held up by a woman servant. As she went up, she glanced over and saw me, and froze like a rock. A jagged stone. Only her curious, keen right eye observed me for an instant, like a falcon. Then, without betraying a sign, she resumed her course up the stairs and disappeared beyond the high portal of the college.

That day she was not the only one who made me understand I no longer existed. The notary did, too; he made me wait half a day in the receiving room before finally sending word that he couldn't see me. I was afraid.

The king's and the grand duke's partisans were always at sword's point, although the grand duke hadn't been assassinated yet. If those who hadn't wanted to betray him had gone into exile, those who neither wanted to go into exile nor to compromise themselves pretended ignorance. In fact, we had only one friend, the illustrator in Saint-Eustache; it was he who found work for my mother as an embroiderer for a shopkeeper in his neighborhood.

I left the notary's office and went back toward Rue Saint-Jacques de la Colline. I was calmed; the Saint-Victor abbey, huge and fortified, among the vineyards and fields, seemed another world. I thought of all the rare things and of the books preserved there. I thought that maybe I would like to forget everything and to walk inside the abbey, to start over. I could be a student there and one day walk proudly into the Tavern du Mulet and mingle among the professors and students. I know it was really a ridiculous idea, but it came to mind because that day I had to escape reality, had to imagine ridiculous things.

I thought, Now that I am just beginning to understand the facts of the city so obviously exposed, now that I am beginning to understand what really counts in the logic, cunning, and vitals of a human body, no one will listen to me any more. Who am I now? Nothing. Nobody. I no longer belong to the calling-card circuit. Fortunately—I immediately thought—I am lucky to have escaped this massive absurdity, the absurdity of having to discuss absolutely useless things as if they were relevant.

I was alone, and conscious of my uniqueness, of how I'd learned to glimpse what's real. Yet, walking back on my route that day, everything was truly beautiful. The hill, the line of almond trees, the sound of lutes. Everything appeared harmonious.

But something stronger, tenacious, and obsessive, something like the echo of a distant insurrection, haunted me. Those towers and all those luxurious wares hid ignorance; they were moribund and their worth only relative. That perfumed gentleman who walked toward me with his entourage of valets enriched himself by grabbing inheritances, by demanding his percentages, by having a rival assassinated, and paying his workers miserable wages. Why do people gather around the forger exposed to the crowd with the counterfeit money hung around his neck?

Ever since I was born there had been battles and wars, festivals and spectacles. They used to display copper pitchers and silver plates, precious embroidery, and oriental rugs just as cheerfully as they displayed decapitated, burned, and dismembered cadavers. So, I said to myself: You don't deceive me any more. I no longer believe. I only want to know if there is anything that doesn't fake goodness, that doesn't fatten evil, doesn't die, putrefy, or camouflage itself as something it isn't. That's all I want to know. And I don't want to waste time.

At the market by the bridge exit, I heard the harsh voices of people selling trout and dried herring alternating with the poultry butchers' cries. If you pay the toll you have the right to leave one world and enter another. What a world it is! Made up of abuses, illusions, and ignorance. Deceived by the powerful. But, how is one to escape this long war, this century?

*　*　*

We had two little rooms with a tiny window. We shared an entrance with the neighbors as well as the kitchen and courtyard. My mother worked as an embroiderer for a tailor who did up hand purses and fancy clothes. Nostalgic for a better past, she worked silently, sometimes at home, sometimes in the shop.

In those days, after I had put the house in order, I went to visit the market or the chapel, although, really, I looked for any excuse to get out of our rooms. Through the streets I went, past the markets and the garbage piles where the pigs rooted, toward the Porte Saint-Antoine. Sometimes I went that far even though in winter the roads were muddy.

Every day new groups of people from the country arrived. Surrounded by a crowd, they told long stories, imparted information, and complained. They talked about bad crops, enemy troops, and mercenaries. They foraged, trying to escape from the reprisals of war, from plague. There was one man who had been on the road for months, and there were groups of pilgrims that were always on the move despite everything, and you didn't know if they told the truth or invented everything. They told about rough, rocky roads, distant trails, and immense cathedrals, of the Pape de la Lune—one of the dissident popes—and of the councils.

To me, the distant routes seemed a spider's web of crossings and deaths; this one died before he reached that valley, so-and-so fell in an ambush by brigands before reaching such and such a city, on and on. That year more than a thousand groups had left from here for Compostella, but only an exhausted, tatterdemalion remnant got back to the city. The crowd looked admiringly at their staffs and their scallop-shell necklaces.

In the two years following the death of my father, I suffered less. I was free, less troubled. I wanted to know more. I didn't find anyone who might help me, but reality itself was a form of revelation, a drama of meanings to unravel. I thought about things, talking to myself in a low voice as I walked or sat at home at my window. In the winter I couldn't open it, but a diffuse, yellow light came in through the oiled cloth.

I had time.

I no longer had to study, pray, make plans for a future that didn't interest me, or seek explanations for things in which I no longer believed. I was caught up in my own meditations and completely alone. What else could matter to me? Even reading had become irksome; but by this time I was no longer allowed to have either books or tutors. It was better this way; I preferred to wander. Life eased up, like a contracted muscle lets go.

So, when I could, I went out. There were the jugglers who

came every so often to put on shows along the streets. They laid a canvas on the ground, held down by stones placed in a row, and there they displayed their objects. One drank some boiling water and immediately spit out cold water before a stupefied public. Another opened his throat to the sky, unsheathed a sword and swallowed it. Only the sword's handle remained visible. We were up close and there was no doubt it wasn't a trick. Then he pulled the sword out very slowly and, after he had those next to them touch the sword, he bowed and calmly sat down. There were trained monkeys, and tumblers said to be from Egypt. They were dressed in cloth that was dyed, cut, and resewn randomly. They lined up; the smallest mounted on the heads and shoulders of the largest, and so forth. Then, at an agreed-on sign, they clapped their hands and jumped, somersaulting in the air.

I watched these things with rapt attention. I thought they were marvelous; the ability to use the body as a tool in intimacy with the unknown thrilled me. The fact that a person might make the body, gestures, and objects so highly manageable seemed important. The jugglers and tumblers, I thought, certainly were closer to understanding the body and its nature, closer to the supernatural than were the spectators encased in thick gristle, who were somewhat affected but prone to soon forget what they saw.

Often, at such times, all the bells were struck, and everyone closed their stores and ran to see what had happened. Who died? The king was in danger? The English had come? A peace treaty was signed? There was a plague? Then someone would begin to stir people up, priming them for a celebration. But there was no salt, no bread. Wheat cost triple what it would have cost before my father was killed, and people boiled cabbages and turnips. Many continued to arrive from the countryside, massing along the convent's walls or around the central markets, waiting for work, or simply waiting for a handful of beans.

Then there were all the bands of beggars, cripples and vagabonds, and all those little children that went around in groups among the garbage and refuse. How many of them died every night? That year, the year when the river flooded and the cold was terrible the wolves came right into the city. During the forty days of Lent, the evangelists in the squares multiplied and even came here to the middle of the cemetery, railing against luxury. Against folly. They exhorted people to repent. Hundreds of penitents lined up along the streets. They came slowly, barefoot, wailing, black hoods shrouding their faces, shoulders bared, and they wore long, white skirts. They flagellated themselves with small, light whips. The crowd followed them, one person swiftly collecting the blood-soaked mud.

It was raining, and how long it had rained. The whole city was miserable and had an empty stomach. Everyone had pallid faces and parched mouths, and moved like automata, even at vespers. In the evening no one dared to go out. They closed the big gates and put up chains around the quarters; whoever had no home or refuge was trapped like a hare hunted by hounds. Many died every night of hunger, cold; people were drowned, devoured, assassinated. Here in the cemetery they put everyone in a common grave. Even the old sacristan made business selling their fat, their teeth, and their hair.

My life was truly changed. When our room became dismal, suffocating, full of foul vapors, then I went out if I could. Like one comes out of a mother's womb—breathing. I went to those places with which a particular detail had made me familiar, and where I was able to breathe a little clean air, see plants, and sit to watch without being recognized. When I grew calm, I went back home. I worked at whatever was at hand, cleaned, mended clothes, and put in order the few manuscripts and letters I still had. Although I no longer studied, some things I had read or heard read would come back to me, and now I understood them more clearly. I saw them in both their intrinsic and relative dimensions, as if they had been arranged in a strange geographic order in my mind. And I understood that living this way—in this void I had created—something was beginning to happen. I had to keep myself in readiness.

Here among the cemetery's arcades I discovered a votive fresco. They told me it was a fresco a philosopher had commissioned in honor of his alchemist wife, who had died many years ago. Her name is written at the bottom. Go look at it yourself. Yes, it's there, beneath the ossuary, beside the Arcade de la Vierge. My memory is not mistaken, how could it be? I went there so many times.

If you look from the bottom to the top, the first picture shows the Slaughter of the Innocents under the eyes of Herod on his throne. The soldiers hold the bloody children by their feet. At the sides are dragons, one winged and one not; then some votive figures, the alchemist Nicolas Flamel and his wife Pernelle Flamel, and their protector. There are hermetic sentences, in Latin. One reads, if I'm not mistaken: *"vere illa die terribilis erit."*

Draped in yellow linen, Christ stands at the center.

At the beginning it was impossible for me to look at this fresco because of the Slaughter of the Innocents. But then one day I heard some people discussing the meaning of these scenes. Someone maintained that the innocents killed by Herod were to recall the corporeal transmutation of metals that dissolve, and Christ represented the gold of knowledge and philosophical wisdom. The resurrection scene of two men and a woman standing half-naked in a coffin represented, he said, the reawakening of the body, spirit, and soul. The winged dragon stood for light substances, and the one without wings, for heavy substances. From that day I continued to return; I sat at a distance and waited. Often there were passing pilgrims who spent the night under the arches. When no one was there at certain times of the day, I got closer. I stood leaning against the columns. To tell the truth, I liked to look at these painted images.

Once, as a young girl, I had a dream. I was facing a window in a room lit with a torch even though outside it was day, but a wan, lead-gray day. The sun came up and the sky became radiant with yellow, pink, and pale blue light; in the distance, among the mountains, appeared a slender figure who walked swiftly. In a few seconds he crossed the valley and the plain along a curved road and came toward me. He was a young man dressed as a page in tight-fitting stockings and a jerkin decorated with silver. As he came toward me, the colors grew more intense and crystalline. The room grew steadily darker. Rushing toward me, B.—which he told me was his name—said to me, "Get up, come, we're going. I came to get you. I have many things I am going to show you." Then I flew, just so, through the window, leaving behind me an empty room. Something in the colors of the fresco and the painted figure of the woman half out of the coffin made me recall this dream, a journey from dark to light.

I remember that in that last year each moment of every day and each stage of the seasons were sublime. They seemed magical to me. I was seized by an ardent craving, a frenzy, a strange nostalgia for nature. Yes, the longing for something indescribable. In May I went as far as Porte Saint-Martin, and without daring to go out—the war was still going on—I looked at the distant forest and fields. Modest processions of the faithful slipped out quickly to bless the crops. The people gathered under the temple wall. Some improvised speeches; others went about dancing in the gardens and markets. There was a festive air. Where the grass had pushed up enough, they raised the wreathed Maypole. People stayed out in the open air all day long, eating in small groups, and they went back home at sunset with bundles of grass and garlands on their heads. They were seized by the same turmoil as I: to forget everything, the misery, the uncertainty, the rage. We wanted to take advantage of this strange pact with nature on the first sunny days after that terrible winter.

The rich raised tents in their own gardens, banners and ensigns fluttering above their walls. One felt like singing again. The minstrels drew a crowd. It seemed impossible. The city was awakening in its own way—the people put on spectacles and dances. The number of wandering peddlers grew, coming from who knows where, and went about hawking fabrics, baskets, firewood, garlands of leaves, and cakes, their paths crisscrossing along the streets. There was a group that carried the Wheel of Fortune, and the crowd stopped at each crossing. People wanted a reliable sign of destiny.

For a few days I joined some neighbors who went as far as the hillsides where the mills were, rashly challenging the brigands who infested the countryside outside the city walls. We went up and up green paths, still wet, up small roads that seemed of another world. Was I born in a different epoch from theirs? The vegetation had a history different from the one I knew, but I wanted to learn it in all its details. I wanted to come tumbling back down the hill as I did when I was a child, to escape completely from the city, from everything that stole my space, from what inexorably made me grow up. And I thought that now everything must stop. The green must stay like it is, always damp, always warmed by the sun. We are tumbling outside the wheel.

In June, during the festival of Saint Jean, I went with these same neighbors as far as Notre Dame cathedral on the island. The bridge was heavily crowded that day—we didn't have to pay the toll; and they were selling dry figs, Saracen grapes, spices, and dried herring without adding on the city tax.

An enormous crowd came to watch the Mystery Play. The actors were dressed like people of old, some had masks and some turbans; they took their places on the raised, wooden platform erected in front of the main gate. In the string of stalls, between the tents, flowers, and painted, papier mâché columns, there were Adam and the Old Testament prophets, and also scenes of the flight into Egypt and of the Passion. Some actors recited by singing, others stood still and silent. We all watched, astonished; people never tired of circling around, front and back, asking: "Who is that? Who is that other one?" For those who could read, signs with names written on them identified the persons and the cities.

We stayed there all day; the weather was warm and the sky cloudless. When there was a respite, people ate roasted chickpeas and drank water from the copper cups of wandering vendors. When evening came, the crowd dispersed, content that the spectacle would continue for three more days.

The troupe of actors who specialized in the Mystery Play was very popular at that time. I remember that along the street we met the Pharaoh with the glued-on beard who was strolling home, and another actor, still dressed in his ancient costume, who'd left to join his guild's lunch after having played his part. It seemed we could master our destiny. If only people could have grasped the meaning of all this, because we are all, at one and the same time, both the representation and the represented, mirrored images—doubles, triples.

So many years ago. But how many? Now time is contracted like a circle, a disk of which I am the epicenter, from which I have summed up all the distances. Beyond this wall Herod commands that the killing continue, you understand? But here, where I am, time exists. I can spend days and months feeling it; I say "feeling it" because it is a sentiment and a sensation, close to being a vision. Because "it is not," I, existing, can materialize it.

How to explain the feeling of materializing what "is not"? Is it a boundless thing? When I was a child I asked myself if the world is contained in the heavens, and the heavens in the seven spaces, what contains the seven spaces? Where lies eternity? Then I felt as if I were sinking in quicksand. I felt choked, as if I would burst for being incapable of imagining such a thing. And finally I understood that it's not a question of imagining but of feeling, of feeling with all your body and with your mind opened wide like a fan.

I imagined belonging to another time, that my terrestrial time—packed with memories, events, persons, things—is inserted into the cycle of all times. A time of images both imagined and imagining. I remember certain lights and certain distances, and in order to remind myself exactly of when I was a girl, long before the years crowded with nightmares began, I bring back to my mind certain sensations again. Of pebbles underfoot in the fields, of clover eaten and chewed at length, slowly. Invariably, each time the same taste permeated my mouth, a sour, green taste.

But then, was it really I who spent her childhood in the countryside before the war?

Yes, certainly, because sensations and memories of them, the odors and the tastes of which they are composed, are proofs of it. I know a secret place behind the hill! I can think back to its precise details, surprising them like mislaid, diluted visions, yet absolutely intact. They drift in space. I left them behind a while ago. When? But now, of course! Distances are cancelled, even if turning back is impossible.

Feeling is what allows the luminous body to alter terrestrial time, to break the cycle of personal time.

Many years earlier, I'd fallen in love with a young student. He left during the war, went back south, beyond Aquitaine. He'd come to my father for work in his free time, to copy manuscripts or put the accounts in order. He'd often go with me to public talks in the lecture hall of his college. We felt alike, and spent a lot of time together. Something in him was very strong and at the same time very fragile. He was removed, gripped by a strange feeling for life, an intense, tenacious emotion, which I'd never seen in anyone else. Now I have a similar feeling—about everything, what's in the air, on earth, beyond the horizon.

For a very brief time I forgot the wretchedness and sadness. This period ended with the beginning of that winter; it was the year the grand duke was assassinated, and the city was oppressed again by the terror of persecution and by completely unbridled intrigues. Although no one in our quarter had had the time to bother with me, my mother didn't approve of my life. She couldn't resign herself to the idea that her only daughter, still young, who, despite misfortunes, nevertheless would have been able to marry well, had become an obsessive, a mantled figure who went out only to trail the penitents and kept the company of eccentric people without a future.

So, one day she remarried, to a cloth merchant. This gentleman came to talk to me. He was fat, old, wore a fur beret and a lined cape. Embarrassed, he sat down on the edge of a chair and, while nervously scratching his belly and picking his teeth, told me that he had married my mother. After all, he said, she was still young, beautiful, and deserved a better life. He was fortunate, he said, that he'd met her. He was a widower, with three children and a large house to look after. As for me, I had become too strange and disrespectful. My place was in a convent; I would be enrolled immediately as a novice with the Sisters of Sainte Catherine.

3

THE BEGGARS' BRAWL

A PILE OF DRY BRANCHES burns at the base of the wooden platform erected in the cemetery clearing. Surrounded by a crowd of people, a preacher from the Mendicant Friars is standing on the wooden pulpit thundering against the rich. He exhorts women to repent and renounce worldly vanity, precious objects, and fine dresses. "Naked we are born and naked we must die," he says. "Richness and conceit blind you, make you foolish, prey of the devil, and lead to eternal damnation!" People warily approach the makeshift pulpit. A young woman takes off her shoes and goes barefoot in the ashes. Other well-dressed women tear off headdresses, discard veils, laces, mother-of-pearl buttons. Someone makes them throw their wigs into the fire. The flames are dense and smoky; a penitent standing nearby swings a censer of burning incense.

"And I say unto you," cries the preacher from on high, "that the fifteen signs of the Apocalypse have already appeared. Do you not see your bodies attacked by leprosy and smallpox? See the death, which must race without ceasing, like the wolves that come in the night even up to your houses? And how those—over there—go around in lined coats and sleeves embroidered with golden threads. Their women, the very likeness of Beelzebub, wear on their heads the devil's two-horned hat filled with lice-infested hair shorn from the dead. And in this very spot they sell fat from cadavers to use as unguent to adorn the skin! Damnation!"

The bells have already pealed three masses but the crowd is still outside in the clearing; people come and go, shout, hypnotized by the crackling flames, listening to the Capuchin friar's sermon, rhythmically underscoring his words with wails and invocations. An hour before sunset, when the cold is no longer bearable, the crowd quickly disperses. Only a small group stays, forming a procession that follows the preacher and heads toward the cemetery exit, beyond the lateral cloisters. For a little while, the banners and the white incense smoke can be made out beyond the surrounding wall as the procession moves away along the narrow Rue des Ferroniers.

The church door is closed. On the opposite side of the cemetery, in the little square between the Virgin's ossuary and the Charnier des Lingères, it is already dark.

Then a whistle sounds.

The Big Turk appears at the far corner of the church wall, crouched over, cautious; he looks around suspiciously from side to side. He squints in order to see better and to ascertain if anyone is coming from that direction. Then, straightening up, he comes forward, supporting himself with a stick. He makes a sign to a group of beggars who come out from behind the corner. Keeping close to the church wall, they pass under the recess, stopping every once in a while to look around, then start to walk again. They reach the Big Turk and stop next to him. There are two young cripples, one of whom drags himself along on two stumps ending at the top of his thighs, and five other hooded men with patched jerkins. No longer hesitating, they head toward the pulpit, where the bonfire had gone out an hour before. Pushing aside little pieces of burnt wood and ashen objects, they look among the remains for something that is still intact—a piece of damask, a button, a needle, a tuft of hair. Anything that can be used, either for itself or to sell.

They stay this way, cautious and bent over the sooty pile, silently stirring the ashes and searching among the carbonized branches.

"Hey!" A nearby shout makes them jump to their feet. "Out! Clear off! This is my turf. We're first. Then you, with my permission, may hunt in the ashes and cinders." With a raucous laugh, a small, thin man comes forward. He is followed by a troupe that forms a menacing circle.

"Ah," notes the Big Turk, "it's you, Gascon. Well, what do you want? We aren't moving from here. We got here first. For this kind of treasure, speed counts, friend. Come closer, come on."

The Big Turk is standing taller than all his companions; covered by layers of rags, he seems still larger. He has a thick, dark head of hair held in place under a hood wrapped with a long scarf that goes under his chin and over his forehead. In his hand he holds a stick smoothed by use, and which he uses to support himself. One foot is missing, but he stands straight and imposing nevertheless. By contrast, the Gascon is bony, with a long, wrinkled face. He doesn't appear to be strong, but can obviously move with agility. His eyes, like an animal's in an ambush, take in everything. No one makes a move to flee. In the half-light illuminated only by two torches near the church, his eyes appear phosphorescent. As if he had set a well-calculated trap, with some quick motions that reveal the nub of his plan, he directs his scroungers to encircle.

He has a company of ten wretches, two, still children, a

cripple, a young idiot, and six men neither young nor old but with a sturdy air despite the rags and the strips of winding cloth. They carry sticks. For some days, they've controlled the part of the cemetery square between the ossuary in the Arcade des Ecrivains and the Fontaine des Innocents, the area of the cemetery most visited. Their only occupation is to collect alms there. This privilege was won in a stick fight after the recent death of Joshua, the strongest of all, and a good friend of the Big Turk. Joshua had kept things in civil order with a certain equity.

"Give me what you're hiding in your sleeves," cries one of the Gascon's group.

"No! It's mine. I saw it when I got here, before anyone else. I'm not giving it up," answers the Saracen, one of the Big Turk's group, retreating, his feet in the ashes. He huddles among his other companions, frightened, bent over with his arms held tightly at his sides.

"Give it to him," shouts the Gascon in a piercing voice, "give it to him or we are taking all your loot, everything you have. And don't raise your sticks at us. Heretical misfits. Bastards. I'm not afraid of you. Go to hell, Big Turk." They look each other in the face, unmoving, taut. The young idiot laughs and in a small, monotone voice repeats, "Coocoo, coocoo, coocoo."

With a nimble jump the Gascon shoves the Big Turk aside and brutally throws the Saracen to the ground. His gangsters follow him and throw themselves on top of the Saracen, trying to pull his arms apart. He is curled up on the ground in the ashes and holds his arms tightly around his chest. In an instant the Big Turk reaches him. He shoves two men aside with his stick, takes another by the throat, and bellows at the Saracen: "Run! Get up, get out of here! I'll take care of these Goths from the wrong side of the Alps!" But the Gascon grabs the young cripple without legs and, seizing him by the waist, cries, "If the Saracen moves, I'll pitch this rotten turnip, this good-for-nothing gnawed core, back into his hole. Listen, I'll have you all smashed flat; anyone who moves."

It is night and, in the dark, the voices seem amplified, more strident. The idiot continues to repeat, "Coocoo, coocoo, coocoo." Then from a distance, from behind the church, comes the glow of a yellow light. Holding a small, smoking torch in his hand, a man runs toward them silently, nimbly. He wears a felt jacket with a hood, foreign trousers tied below the calves with strips of cloth. He has a shoulder bag; his hair is straight and a little long at the sides, cut like a page-boy's. The torchlight makes him copper-colored. In a few seconds the young man reaches the beggars. He takes in the scene

The surprised mendicants are immobilized, as though paralyzed. If at first they squint their eyes to see better and to discern shapes in the shadows, now they stare open-eyed. The yellow flame suddenly, unexpectedly, brings them back to the world of solid, colored outlines. No one makes a sound. One would think they're deaf-mutes as they look at the young man, astonished at his firm voice and deep tone.

"What are you doing, you miserable parasites? Today people put their consciences in order and, in the name of God, threw into the fire what was owed from the beginning, and you kill yourselves here in the name of a lie. What the hell! You're slaves, beasts to the end.

"Where are those people now? Not even the sacristan was awakened by your noise and what you're doing! Fighting each other for a joke? That's a laugh. Tomorrow the whole market will talk about the big fight among a bunch of miserable cripples. Yes, they'll say this, and yes, it will be repeated from market to market by those same gentlemen who threw their furs away, and by those same ladies who tossed their mother-of-pearl on the fire.

"Clear off! If there's blood here now, the guards will come tomorrow and they'll give you another kind of reward. You'll have to pay a fine, or change your territory, or simply be strung up. The church will be closed so it can be reconsecrated. Stupid idiots, beating each other up. In the confusion of war, who cares a fig for you? Be off! The patrol will be here soon.

"Hey, Lombard, who do you take us for, Saint Francis?" laughs one of the beggars.

"No, no, he's right," says the Gascon, all of a sudden strangely conciliatory. "Let him alone, we're going away. Take the Saracen with you."

* * *

The Lombard is seated under the arches. It's already late. In a little while the midday bell will sound, he thinks. The market is at its busiest. He can hear the cries of the merchants coming in from behind the city wall. The Lombard is somber; his feet bared to the sun seemed to be the only living part of his body. He is young, and his dark and shining eyes illuminate his fair face with their penetrating gaze. The Big Turk and the

Lombard's other companions are seated next to him.

"Well then, where's the Gascon?" the Lombard asks the Big Turk.

"I don't know. Like I told you before, I saw him this morning just at sunrise when he found the Saracen dead. He picked him up, carried him behind the bushes, and took off his clothes. But he didn't find anything. Then he hid him farther back in the bushes, took his rags. He stayed around, rummaging and going through the Saracen's things, looking for valuables. But then I didn't see him any more."

"He found the loot!" bawls one of the beggars.

"Not at all!" answers another, "what treasure do you think he might have found? Nothing, that's what. Maybe some fleas, nothing more. I'm absolutely positive. I saw him. I saw the Saracen the night he was about to die. He went hmm . . . hmm . . . . groaning like that, and he groaned for hours, then still more, and faster. After that, he raised an arm, took a ring from under his armpit, put it in his mouth and swallowed it. He said his Jesus-and-Mary and died. The sun was already up. A little later the Gascon found him."

"And you, what did you tell him?" asks another beggar.

"For God's sake, nothing. Otherwise the Gascon would have cut open his stomach. When it comes to precious objects or money, he loses his head. And then what difference is it to me? Death is death and Jesus-and-Mary is Jesus-and-Mary. The Saracen always gave me some crusts and he was as miserable as we are. Treasure! Treasure! There's no treasure here. If we had found treasure would we have rotted away for a piece of bread? We would be like Croesus in his Court."

"Well put!" exclaims the Big Turk.

"The Saracen hid lice, that's what," says another mendicant, laughing. "Those with the gold are those over there. And those others, including the alchemist-professors who go to Pernelle's tomb. They make money, then organize their own funerals and, with a new name, go away to the East and live for a thousand years."

"And we, who never have a calm day, nor an hour without fear, we who never have any relief from our misery, what can we do about it? Tell me, what are you looking so maudlin for?" another asks the Lombard.

> Let the Lombard go his way!
> Don't you see he's overwhelmed
> by his devotion and made weak
> by good intentions? "Your stink,"
> he'll say, "is not from being hungry
> but comes straight from your soul
> —and from that endless fart
> the Devil sends your miserable heart."

The Big Turk mimes these verses, declaiming them in a falsetto voice between the beggars' guffaws. The Turnip rolls on the ground with tears in his eyes. They all clap their hands. The Big Turk takes a couple of dance steps, waving his stick in the air, then, limping down the road, he continues:

> As for us, our choice is this
> it's the abyss of the damned
> with garbage as our grave,
> or it's dangling by our necks,
> turning scabby, black, and dry,

hanging like rats 'long Cuckold's Way
hair shorn, skin gone—old turnips
left out to rot, just skulls and bones

He goes toward the booths of the soup vendors under the Charnier de la Vierge. When he passes under the cell of the walled-in woman, the Big Turk stops, makes a little skip and bows, then continues down the road, chanting:

My dear lady I salute you
how are you faring in that cell?
the confessor's not for you, nor
the priest with his salvation
nor sacristan with bread and water.
You want to wander, all alone,
to daydream.
You want to philosophize,
alone, to see from your cell's slit
this great dark pile of shit
heaped high against the walls
under arch-ribbed market halls
among bare bones, and dry.
But if it's true that I must die
then it's with you that I desire
to spend my days in Paradise!

"Oh! Oh, yes!" says one of the beggars, who turns to the Lombard. "The Big Turk is a true master. When he was young he knew how to read and write—really. Later on, he might have forgotten how. But he's a master. Before Joshua died, they used to sit here and tell stories and make verses. One began and the other followed. They improvised, they did call-and-response and people came out of curiosity to listen to them. There was always a little crowd around them, not only beggars. At the end, if they earned something—because this is how they made a living—they gave everybody a cup of soup.

"There, you see the Big Turk over there, toward the soup vendors' stalls. Soup, hot soup. But the Big Turk can't give it to everybody like he did once; he has no money. He's not clever at asking for alms and doesn't control his territory as well.

"Yes, it's a dog's world. If Joshua were alive, everything would be different. He always had money. The rumor was that he was a magician, a philosopher who manufactured gold. They even say it's not true he's dead, but that he went far away. Others say he gave the money to the sacristan to bring about certain things.

"But don't look at me like that, Lombard, for Christ's sake, I'm only saying what I heard."

During this whole time, the Lombard sits silently, listening without speaking. He remotely follows the coming and going of the people around the soup vendors' stalls. Then he asks, "Who's in that cell?"

"Ah," answers one of the mendicants seated next to him, "the great gentleman finally wakes up. Hey, Lombard, you don't like our company? What's it to you who's down there? You'll never see her, just like none of us has ever seen her. Only Joshua, who was here for years, told us about having seen her in person when she was walled in."

"The whore! She looked very young. Some said she was very ugly, others said she was very beautiful. I myself don't remember," says a beggar.

"The sacristan told us," adds another of the group, "that she was a young nun who chose to be walled in out of devotion. He swore it; that's what he said."

The first beggar bursts out laughing, "Walled in for devotion my ass! That young woman was supposed to be burned as a heretic and sinner, then at the trial she played it smart and here she is. And maybe it's not true she's always in there; maybe at night she goes out by a secret door!"

"You ask me what's her name? Who knows," answers the other mendicant. "But what do you care? A name, a name's useless. Who knows it? Maybe the Big Turk knows it. Or perhaps the Procuress. She knows everything. Yes, the old one down there, the one who was born here. Her mother had just been buried when the Procuress came into this world with a lusty cry. By all the saints! Think of it, born from a double hole, from a fresh grave. Born from heaving soil! Ha!" He laughs and everybody laughs with him. They all get up and leave.

The Lombard sits by himself now. The sun is warming his legs; the shade shifts with the rotating shadows of the arcade's columns. Unmoving, he accepts the bright invasion of his body. The walled-in woman, who could she be? How could she decide to do it? It probably happened in a moment of conviction; certainly she can't have had doubts. You need a cursed conviction in order to turn the world inside out, to put the inside out and the outside in. I only know that I don't know where to search any more, that I don't have the strength. I set out, I begin again, start over. Yes, it's true, I'd like to change, to blow up this miserable life, redo all life's reckonings, all laws. Is it possible that all that counts in the end is the cemetery? That the cemetery is the greatest and mightiest, the recapitulation of everything that happens in the world and in life?

But you, the Lombard mentally asks the walled-in woman, where did you find this conviction? Tell me, whatever did you glimpse, what did you discover? The ideal conditions for philosophizing—can it be possible?—are in a cell! I have traveled everywhere, and everywhere I found misery and calamities. Everything needs remaking, entirely. And that's the reason I go on trying to understand *how,* because if the saints don't do it—and the powerful people never will—we'll do it ourselves. So my grandparents told me when I was little. "Don't even believe in the saints," they said, "believe only in yourself, in yourself and in written words."

I thought about these things one day while journeying with a group of merchants through the mountains in the east toward the free lands. We had been walking with the mules since dawn along the steep roads among forests already completely yellow and red with autumn. The mules were loaded, the weapons ready, and the border passes stamped. But these would be of no use if you happened to meet brigands; shooting is shooting and at that moment you are alone. Parchment, the writing no one reads, customs ink and stamps are of no use. You have to fight, or you'll end up hanging from a tree.

Thank goodness, we came to a safe haven. From afar, we saw the river and the fortified walls of the monastery on the valley floor, and we met three men on horseback. That time we didn't have to fight. They were young, armed peasants heading west. Two days before, brigands had attacked their group, just as they were returning home from the grand duke's fair. The thieves took all their animals and their earnings, burned their tools and killed many of them. This happened before the arrival of the escort promised by the grand duke for their protection. In fact, the soldiers had tarried on purpose and had not even helped them bury the dead.

At least that's what the three young men said while they talked to us from the cliff above. One of them said they were going toward the Black Mountains, beyond the wide river and wintry lands, in order to reach bands of fellow countrymen in revolt. With horses and weapons, these bands attacked the brigands so they could recover their goods. Also, he added, they attacked the king's taxmen, nobles, and soldiers if they had to. With this war without end, who knows who defends the law and the public good and who assaults them? So, he said, the rebels are doing this and doing it well.

"We are going to avenge ourselves by Saint-Elie des Champs; we are fed up with being treated like beasts, always being what the king wants us to be—mute, forever mute. So, I said to my brothers, why are we always growing crops, reaping, driving our animals down there in the summer if after that they come and destroy everything and slaughter us? If it isn't brigands, it's the nobles themselves who seize our tools. How do they think we plow the ground? With our teeth? Our fingernails? Then I told my brothers, we're going. We, too, are going to get ourselves a horse, weapons, helmets, and we're going as far as the mountains in the south. We're putting an end to this!"

He talked to us while keeping a leveled slingshot in hand, and his brothers held two others at the ready. "Just go," he said. "We aren't going to attack you. Give us a horse and some food. And tell the count's men that as long as they are allied with the brigands we are allied with the devil. Saint Elie, isn't he the patron saint of craftsmen? And aren't we craftsmen, masters of our own hands in this damned pit of hell!"

Going down the slope toward the count's lands, I thought about that young man with the slingshot. He really believed that he would reach the Black Mountain bands. He didn't know it would be impossible. The mountains were far away, and he would have to cross two borders, pay various tolls, escape the taxmen, soldiers, and rogues. He would have to fight against lances and wolves. With slingshots? Only with luck. With the help of the saints, one of them had said. But if the saints were against him?

I looked at them, with their bandits' hats, on horses put to gallop. One of them had said, "a bandit is not a brigand; he has morals and a will. He fights against injustice because he has to take care of himself, and he shouts it from the rooftops. A different world wouldn't need bandits."

And I thought, my God, they're right, with the life they lead, who wouldn't revolt?

It's like having yourself walled in. One has to make a definitive decision. If there are no saints, well, we have to make crucial decisions here where we are. But I'm straying from the subject.

Two days later, in the public square of the village of Saint-Laurent du Pont, one of the brothers was hanged, his hands and feet cut off and displayed at the city gates. He'd been caught by the king's soldiers who were coming down the river escorting skiffs loaded with goods.

The other brothers, I don't know. I can imagine all the possibilities, but I will never know if that's what happened to them or if they died of the cold at the ford, or were hanged like thieves in some other village. How can we change habits, think anew about all the powers assembled to keep the dagger at our throats—the pitchforks, the laws, and all the writings codifying them, all the things discovered for improving us and then using them in order to trap us?

We need something more than the air we breathe, something more than the dirt in the fields. What's needed is something like a miracle that totally, imperceptibly, unknown by anyone, invades our skin and bones and will totally transform us. An authentic mutation. A transmutation. These imbecile beggars; they can ruin everything in a flash. They forget we're human beings. If we forget that, there will be no transmutation. The heavens watch us, send us signs, messages, and reach out to us to transform us. But how? Damn, I don't know.

There—there is the low Mass, and over there, the common grave—and I in the midst of life, half living, half dead. I just have to think that young man was right. The bandit's hat is a mark to make him stand out in that damned madhouse. It's a foothold, an idea. A flag, a standard.

But if the bandit were the hat and not the man? Then putting it on would be to change identity, it would be the hat's affair, and he would no longer be just himself on a horse, wearing a hat.

Objects are suspect, terrifying. When I see the gentlemen all dressed up in boots, with a fine chain tied around their calves to lift their boots' long, limp toes so they won't trip, then I can't think that it's a man plus such and such an object, a garment; but, instead, I think, man has become one of the garment's emanations. You, woman, sealed in the wall, are alone in your cowl. It was your way of challenging all the objects and saying the game of objects is over; let's put men and women on one side and objects on the other. Let's begin the game of true life for all us honest people.

Now I don't remember too well, but wasn't it my Waldensian grandfather who talked to me like this? When I was young I went with my father on his trips; the distances then were short—the Lombard region, the villages on the mountains, the visits to the Waldensian families. After he died, I left and began to travel long distances by boat, or in caravans. I crossed many borders, saw so many things; but finally everything looked alike. Yes, this was the strangest sensation. For many years the customs were new, the faces always distinctive, marvelous. Then, one day, things began to look alike. They always had the same stamp on them, I thought. Thank God those days are over.

Now I travel and move in a great circle, but not to be astonished or amused. When I first went to Turkey, I really felt I was traveling, moving in another realm. My eyes didn't tire of observing; everything seemed extraordinary to me, beautiful, fresh. Now, instead, I observe from the depths with a different eye, one hidden in my guts. I'm no longer able to let myself go like I once did. When we sang and lit the fire, bedding down, then I was happy. I listened to stories of other journeys ever more extraordinary and I felt good.

Now I move in a circle. Arriving, I find myself; leaving, I pursue myself. I no longer try to discover anything; I only observe what happens in front of me, what hunts me down, while it comes together like a forgotten puzzle. Each day I discover a different scene, yet one that existed before. Say that it's the *outer* that discovers me and travels in me. I have become a vast world.

No, it's not that beautiful and marvelous things no longer surprise me. It's as if, in tacit agreement, I had existed forever with the sky, the earth, those unexplored fords that were there before our caravan passed, and will be there forever. At the same time, I am an old acquaintance of atrocities and lies. No, we don't discover the other. I spy on their ambush, they on my wandering.

Yes, it was my grandfather who told me about the Perfect Ones of the Cathars, a heretical sect that existed in and around Toulouse, before being exterminated more than a hundred years ago. But I don't enjoy his certainty. I have doubts, and don't know how to find solutions. I can't keep on for another twenty years—if that's how long I've already lived—following the wheel's turning. Finally, you put yourself in the center pivot and say "Enough!" There you stay, immobile, and at the same time move, as if you were standing in the midst of a cyclone, or a waterspout, a corridor binding heaven and earth.

They say there's calm there in its center. If that's true, then I understand. I understand why I chose to come to this very spot, here in the Cemetery of the Holy Innocents, the most putrid whorehouse in this city, in this entire country. Only la Cour des Miracles off Rue des Feuilles Sèches is worse. No, I never went there; not even the seneschal's policemen go there. It's a kingdom with its king, Croesus and his *papesse*. An anti-kingdom, a model fortress. An inferno.

But then, where is the eternal and mighty kingdom that is

promised to us? There can be nothing mightier than this king, than this rotting soil.

*   *   *

"Good Lord, Lombard!" the Big Turk interrupts suddenly, sitting down beside him, "you're always silent, always thinking. But do you never sing? No? Fart, belch, shit, my God, do something! Stop thinking, for your own good. You're pale from too much thinking. Who knows how many useless things, how many stupidities, with respect to . . . .

"Come on, eat some chickpeas. Everybody here eats chickpeas. I am the master of the chickpea eaters. Haven't they told you?

"May I sit down? Yes? Here, take some, come on. You were very clever yesterday, really. Sentimental as you are, you saved us from an awful beating.

"I knew that the Gascon, rotten liar and villain like everybody from Gascony, had planted three rogues who waited for his signal to catch us. He'd set a trap, honestly, he who thinks himself the captain of who knows what war. But you, with your tender heart, saved us. It's true; we would all have been slaughtered, as if we weren't crippled or hard up enough as it is.

"I'm big, I make people afraid, but I'm not going to come to blows. I prefer to make poems. When Joshua was still around, we sat by each other to tell stories. Even clever Joshua—like all of us—was lost in this circus of stinking bones. He knew how to make poetry, knew how to read and write. He would start, and I would follow up, and everybody would gather around to laugh and listen, yes, to weep also sometimes when Joshua talked about certain things. He had no equal.

"He stood there, the Saracen next to him. Joshua threw out a verse, tossed out another one. When nobody expected it, the Saracen recited the poem he'd composed. He too was a poet, a poetaster. He was one of us, rejected and abandoned. He had been brought here as a slave by a Venetian merchant; and here he was, planted like a barren bush in this cemetery, this sanctuary and refuge without a name. God, what a fate! In a Christian country, a country of brutes and sacristans.

"The Saracen earned some money by keeping the mules and asses of the gentlemen peaceful when they came to Mass. When these beasts were nervous, tired, or hungry like we are, he was the only one who understood them and knew how to make them be still with a sharp "Frrr," or with a pat of understanding accompanied by a loud "Frrr." At times he gave them something to drink, and there was always a pile of straw ready at hand on the ground.

"And that's how it happened. Dead from the blow of a fist for a ring that was probably just copper. What's certain is that he swallowed it to make sure it wouldn't fall into the Gascon's hands to be sold for gain. Doesn't the proverb say, 'When the money stops trouble starts?' A man like the Saracen would never sell a ring; if he swallowed it, he had his reasons.

"Christ, the Gascon and his cronies always insulted him and made fun of him! They hung around to spy on him in order to rob him of the money he earned. I don't know how those people who spy on you for coins track you down when you're dog-tired. From far off, their ears quiver at the jingle of two coins. The Gascon and his gang are greedy for money. But we, we always paid everybody for good hot soup, and we repaired some of the less-patched sandals, expecting a cold winter and harsher days when almost no one comes here and some people die of hunger and frost.

"So, they made fun of the Saracen, laughed at him because of that hole he had here in the middle of his nose, his Venetian owner's mark. The slave's stigma. They'd put a little ring in the lobe of his nose; but I don't know what became of it, really, because I always saw him with that empty hole, from the side and against the light. Maybe it was because of that he thought of holding onto the ring he'd found? Maybe a way of redeeming his slavery. Damn, even if he'd been able to, one slavery followed another. For people like him and me, the entire world is a big dealer.

"They laughed and laughed, but he was serious, always sober. At bottom he was stronger because he never got angry, but yesterday he must have lost patience once and for all. Damn it! Now he's dead, crushed and beaten. And who would have imagined it last night? Probably it was the result of seeing all those sallow gentlemen throwing away buttons and laces, those notaries tearing off their furs, and it really depressed me. Something has to be done, I told myself, to get at least a little of God's goods.

"Lately things are going badly. The Gascon wants to rule everybody and everything and take his cut of all the alms. He wants to be King of the Field, King of this sacred and joyous field! What an honor for him. Damn him! He understands nothing of life, nor death, nor of our poetizing. He shares soup with nobody.

"Friend, I never expected, honestly, I never imagined that the Saracen had to die yesterday. This is a strange unpredictable land. This cemetery is a world, and we are citizens without a city, unmarked and unnamed. Christ, nothing changes. Only one great destination. We take our turn at death and we watch the living. Everybody comes here from the market, the ladies, great and small, citizens, peasants, to relieve themselves shamelessly in the bushes. Who can feel shame in front of the dead? And we are among the dead. But, no question, we see it all, that big world. We get to listen to La Serene and La Bicocque strike all the hours—now a Mass, now a funeral—life is a great uproar of bells and chimes. And we are always in the sun, in the open air, in the rain, always waiting, always ready. Isn't it the same thing? We're a big cemetery in which fleas and lice come and go. We have sores on our skin, unexplored earthly pits and putrefaction. Yes, that's how it is.

"But we're saints, holy and genuine wretches, not like the phony cripples and people with false sores at the court of King Goth or Croesus. They steal children. The break them and put them back together like monsters, then carry them around. They're shameless charlatans. In the evening, they return like worms to Rue du Mur, Rue des Feuilles Sèches, and Impasse du Merry. No, even that court rejects us. We are outcast rabble. Yes, that's how it is.

"But then why do I tell you all these things? You aren't one of us. Look at yourself. A pilgrim you say? But you don't have anything. Where do you think you're going without a hat and no boots? My God, even you, a poetaster too. Come on, forget everything, and get up. We're going to eat a little something. The best fritters in the world come from right here and I've got a few coins.

Come on, Lombard, up on your feet!
Let's eat some chickpeas, have some bread!
Let's toast with soup the memory of a friend
a valiant Saracen from an alien land
now done for in the trenches and, to our surprise
he's most likely on his way to Paradise!

The Big Turk stands up and walks away, the Lombard follow-ing him.

"Come on! Paradise?" says one of the beggars to the Big Turk, taking him by the arm. "Certainly not paradise. The Gascon wants to give us trouble. He told the caretaker that someone's dead and that we killed him in order to rob him. If the guards come and find us, they will take us and throw us all out. We have to hide the Saracen, throw him into a deep hole—my God, it won't be easy—the Gascon has taken the knife to him and made a long slice in him, like this, and pulled out all his guts."

"What are you saying? What the devil—by the holiest Moor—the Gascon did this? How could he? The guts, the guts of a poor devil, the belly of a friend. Where is he? How did this happen?"

The Big Turk curses as he runs. He covers distance quickly, supporting himself with his stick, excitedly waving his other arm, completely forgetting about the Lombard. The beggar and the Turnip follow him. Even the Turnip runs with surprising speed by leaning on two short pieces of wood he holds in his hands, which he uses to raise himself slightly from the ground, progressing with a movement that throws his trunk forward. The three disappear into the distance; you can still hear some words shouted hurriedly, but no one seems to pay attention. No one turns their head.

This cemetery is engrossed in who knows how many other dramas, the Lombard thinks to himself. Who knows how many things happen here that I don't know. How strange this Big Turk is, a beggar who seems like a corsair, but a redeemed corsair. "Redeemed," I don't know why this word comes to mind. From what must he be redeemed? I don't know. But certainly he's freer than I. I'd like to talk to him, like to ask him to tell me about this place. I'm sure he knows many things. But that wind today, look at all this dust in the air. It's strange. It's a summery wind, yet this is still March. The bursts of hot air make me feel something dry and sultry. It comes from afar and carries smells of grass and embryos, of pollen, living smells in a dead lea. A troubled wind, corsair and curser, it stirs the dust between tombs and pits, abates and then goes, starts up again, begins to blow again. Yes, I will ask the Big Turk to sit down beside me, ask him to talk to me.

4

LA DANSE MACABRE

THE BIG TURK LIMPS along toward some tents in the wide clearing.

The Lombard follows him. He's worried: And if, starting from yesterday, I'd been reborn like a serpent that sheds its old skin? After all, I've been here only a few days, temporarily lodging under the arcades, waiting for the pilgrims to gather. But this week is like being on a precipice. I feel like I'm living something that happened before and that I had to get to. I feel like somebody who's made a long trip, crossed a difficult pass over a chain of mountains and finds himself where another slope begins: A peak and two paths, an earlier one and this one, and I'm on both at the same time. If I thought I was safe and sound now, I was wrong.

He, too, heads toward the tent and goes in.

In the cold night, the tent gives the reassuring sensation of warmth. It's made of stiff, unbleached canvas, octagonal at the bottom, pointed at the top. It seems small, about fifteen feet high; and it's filled with people. There are stools all around and some mats in the middle. Two hunched painters are putting finishing touches on the details of a screen. A young man insistently repeats a motif on his fife as his cheeks puff up like two little balls made of skin, alternately taut and flaccid.

Seated on a taller stool, a monk talks to an actor and to a tall, thin man with a long face and pointed nose. The Big Turk has already taken his place at the side, among the curious, and seems happy. He grabs the Lombard's arm and bending toward him, whispers, "Ah, these are true poets. Listen, Lombard. That one down there is the Moor, the other the friar. Shhh, listen, the rehearsals are beginning. Those women down there are from the company. No, they aren't what you think. They left everything—home and family—and joined the group, traveling with it from Aquitaine. Sit down, damn it! Shhh."

There is an air of expectancy. Someone distributes bowls of hot soup that everyone passes around, taking sips. Then the friar rises and says: "And at this point the three Marys enter and say, 'And who are you?'"

"But why the three Marys?" someone asks.

"Because they went about in search of the tomb, in search of the holy body so they could wrap it in the burial cloth. It is thus they see death and introduce him," answers the friar.

"But how?" asks another curious person. "Aren't there some monks to play Mary Magdalene and the other Marys?"

Amidst general laughter, the friar answers, "No, for the first time we're giving the parts to three real women. The abbot-transvestite Marys you're used to seeing in our spectacles, with their wigs and their clumsy manners, make people laugh. We want something serious. Only the Jester is to make them laugh.

"They will have dark blue cloaks, the color of night, and hair loosened like virgins; they will have the sadness, the clairvoyance and conscience of the ancient sibylls, three witnesses to the day of resurrection."

The friar speaks on his feet, waving his hands and lowering his voice as if it were a mysterious matter.

"Then I enter," says the Moor, coming forward, "I answer the line and say:

I am the clown, I am the crazy,
I am the blockhead and the obsessed.
I am the conscience of the dead
not the skull, but the living heart of man.
I am the comrade of the missing
the juggler for the great buffoon.
I act out the question, dance the answer
at the threshold of every door.
I summon you and follow the crowd
of the living—and the dead.

And you, down there, lower the sign with the words THE JESTER OF DEATH." He nods to the musician. "You'll play the motif of the Marys three times. And you, Marys, will reappear a little after the scene in order to ask again: 'And You, Who are You?'"

The Moor recites these lines, making little repeated jumps with easy agility. His face is very serious, imperturbable. But the contrast between his dry severity and the expression in his eyes, which roll in an exaggerated manner, cause the listening audience to laugh. But their laughter is filled with dread. This thin man has a sharp, magnetic glance. Leaping like a juggler, he shows great mastery in his gestures and his moves. The Big Turk looks at him in admiration, repeatedly slapping his thighs.

"Lombard, hey, listen. When Joshua was alive it was like this, just like this. We all sat on the ground in a circle and he stood up and told us all an ancient Mystery by himself, with gestures and changes in his tone of voice. Damn! What a fine comrade!

Let's listen. Shhh. What? I? Never say that! I make a verse? Go
to hell! What am I in comparison with these masters?"

The Big Turk makes a gesture, as if he were ashamed of himself. Two beggars call to him in a loud voice, then three, then all
join in with whistles and shouts. "Big Turk! Big Turk!"

The friar stares at him for a moment and then says to him,
"Of course, you—you're from here—give us a strophe, welcome
us as you should!"

Limping and half bent over, the Big Turk stands up; he remains in thoughtful silence for a moment, then takes a deep
breath, making himself even bigger. With a flicker of his eyes,
he looks straight at the audience. He improvises a dance step
and says:

> Dear friars, companions and friends,
> let's not condemn the Truly Blessed
> this grassy soil beneath our feet.
> This earth so heavy, scented sweet
> is like a giant penitent's back
> bearing us up, nobles and wrecks.
> We must dance and sing,
> consult the dead, salute this holy place
> for the thieving and the strong.
> Listen, while I beat out
> a song especially for us.
> Let's face it.
> We're all stirred around in the same stew pot,
> whether handsome or ugly or one of the happy,
> there are winners—and leftover numbers
> drawn from the very same lot.

The Big Turk changes rhythm and pose:

Kings and knaves are almighty,
and so are the knights.
Their winnings are kept in gold,
and in tolls paid by those
who cross their lands.
They're powerful brigands
with untouchable hands.
But two actors,
the Madman and the Fool,
dance our questions boldly,
and the mime responds,
reminding us of who
commands the world."

Then he leans forward and recites:

The Queen of this Home
levels everyone
both rich and humble.
And we, the unrepentant garbage
of the mighty, are here condemned
for their sins. Let's sing
aloud the skirmish for life—
a ballad of those who fight
for glory and for might
while we struggle in this dump—
we beggars and tramps
we who battle with our bellies,
without edicts, without lance.
We fight only with songs and anger,
without horses and always in danger
we fight only with our hunger.

Shouts and applause accompany the Big Turk, who stops
sometimes, half bent forward, balancing with his stick, starting

up again, singing a little, declaiming a little, building the pace. Toward the end, when the rhythm is quickened and more pronounced, the Big Turk is bent completely forward and with his stick beats out his lines on the ground.

Then the Moor pirouettes up to the Big Turk, bows slightly to him, and, turning to the audience, says: "We thank our friend and greet you all. We will do honor to this welcome with the Mystery of the Savior. Come one, come all, day-after-tomorrow. Come all you bright and stupid ones—this jester and the Marys will recite the truth."

The Moor stresses the word "truth," displaying his teeth and knitting his brows.

The clock strikes nine and everybody leaves after another rehearsal and repeated plaudits. People leave the tent hurriedly in little knots. The night is cold and already dark.

"Lombard! What a night! They laughed. They said I was great. Even the gravediggers seemed happy—obviously, with the warmth, the soup, those beautiful women. Christ! Tonight it seemed like another world! Those moments are like rafters in a house; they hold things up. Do you understand?"

Outside the air is cold. It makes you huddle up to protect yourself, but the Big Turk goes right on, feeling light as air, excited by the idea of having done something particularly important. He keeps gesticulating, warming himself while talking. The Lombard nods in order to make him happy, but a strange uneasiness prevents him from talking.

The last light in the tent is now extinguished, leaving only the distant torches, as the lights carried by the departing groups disappear.

Then, before the Lombard can grasp what is happening, the Gascon springs from behind a bush, closes quickly, and strikes the Big Turk from behind with a pointed piece of iron. Without a sound, without a gesture, the Big Turk falls to earth with a moan.

The Lombard would like to pursue the dark shadow that vanishes, but he stays. He stays and bends down. While kneeling, he has the sense that he is going down, as if falling from a roof. He feels heavy, heavy as lead, and then suddenly light. He feels dead and reborn in a fraction of an instant. Oddly, he is sweating; it's cold out but he is sweating. He has the hot sensation of a fire tongue. His stomach tenses. He feels nauseated.

The Big Turk is dying, his breathing raspy. Blood oozes from his mouth. With his finger, the Lombard feels the viscous, lukewarm liquid on the Big Turk's chin.

The Lombard wants to say, "Take it easy! Don't die. Get up and sing something. Like you tell us, we're visible, we exist. You can't die. This foul earth can't take you. None of this is true—it's the friar's stupid joke. He's put you in the Mystery play. It's only your manikin the artist's painted, the meanest scene—just to bring in something for the people to hiss. Don't let yourself be fooled. We're lighting the torches, counting the money. I'm sure we have enough to buy a permit. Get up! No vermin can get near you. Come on, get up, get up!"

But he can say nothing. His mouth is clamped shut, his tongue dry. He just manages to prop up the Big Turk's head comfortably on his legs. Halfway to the ground in the dark, on his knees in the wet bushes, the Lombard can feel the warm, sticky blood trickle slowly down his hand.

Quickly then, he puts his other hand under the rough shirt in a recess of his vest and finds the tattered sack. Clutching it in his palm, he opens it with his teeth, and on a finger brings some salt grains to the Big Turk's mouth, and puts a little under his nostrils. Then he puts the rag, refolded, back in its place.

After a long silence, the Big Turk answers in a deliberate, precise voice—the voice of the versifier, thinks the Lombard. "Good Lombard, you calmed a storm. My God, I see the Great Bear. Honest. I'm on the sea. There's the smell of salt. And with the salt there's also the smell of ginger and resin. These Alpine barbarians, they know nothing. After all, blood is a poor thing; it flows from my veins like the streams that go back to the ocean. Lombard, fart on the devil, as they say. Now, from here, I hear a seashell's sound.

"To you, friend, to you, stranger: Who sees is seen, who hears understands . . . "

5

THE LOMBARD MEETS
THE BOHEMIAN

DISTRACTED AND WITHOUT PURPOSE, the Lombard walks past the cloth merchants toward the huts and the large tent that have been installed in the cemetery clearing.

In the first hut, two artisans and a painter are refinishing the papier mâché heads. Small piles of plaster and paints are placed on the ground on some pieces of cloth; beside them are closed sacks and buckets of pitch, the heads of the Pope, the King, and the Knight. The Knight's head is still unpainted, one eyebrow on, the other not. In a corner, arms and legs are laid out in a line, bleaching. A costumer is re-dressing them with colored material that he sews, adjusts, cuts, and arranges with their matching heads—red taffeta for the Pope, damasked satin for the King, a toga bordered with ermine for the Judge, a cloak of green cloth for the Friar.

The Lombard, musing, goes out and walks to another hut. Two women make their way toward him. One is tall and old. She wears a black, wrinkled skirt, and her head is swathed in a long discolored, yellow veil. She looks at him and says, "You've been here for some days, boy, but I still haven't seen you beg for alms. Who are you? I haven't seen you write letters or do any business. What do you want? A pilgrim—without a hat—how will you make out on the mountain roads? Say! Do you like my daughter? The sacristan always comes looking for her and so do those passing through."

The Lombard gestures vaguely with his hand and notes the young girl standing behind the old woman. The same body, the same stature, but the face is still young. The old one's face is full of wrinkles, ugly lines crystallized into the expression of a rapacious bird. A carnivorous bird. The daughter has a face without history, flat and unexpressive. Her eyes are like two empty holes, vacant, patient, strangely dead.

"No," answers the Lombard, "let me alone. I'm a pilgrim and have vowed chastity."

"Listen, who do you think you are, my handsome one? Do you think I didn't see you yesterday unloading sacks and piles of dirt from a cart in the market? You're a lumper, that's what, not in the least a pilgrim. Chastity, chastity, but what are you telling me? It doesn't exist. That's what I say, I, who know everybody. So serious. Maybe you're just in love; but then who would you love if my daughter here is the most beautiful of all. Maybe you're from a faraway place. You're not likely a condemned priest, and you probably aren't thinking of the holy virgin! No, nor of a little bird in the air. Oh, she's buried here and you came to weep on her tomb or dig up some bones! No? Then she's alive! The abbess? Not her either? It's certainly not the woman in the wall? Ah, that's it then. This is good, really good."

The old hag bends over laughing, her mouth opened on putrefied, black teeth, eyes wrinkled in a convulsive grimace; tears flows from her eyes as she laughs. Composing herself again, she fixes the Lombard with an imperturbable stare and continues speaking to him.

"Serious, you're too serious. Surely you're not searching for treasure? Tell me, I know everything here, pebble by pebble, bush by bush. Really, tell me. I'll help you find where it is. I know the graves; I venture among the bones."

The Lombard draws back, tries to get away, then stops, looks at her and says, "Good, exactly. You tell me. Tell me, who is the woman sealed in the wall?"

"You really are a strange type, asking me about her when I suggest looking for treasure instead; but I'll be patient with you. Look here, to tell you the truth, I don't know who she is; but I remember she's called Alix, and from a good family. The prioress and the judge came with her in person all the way up here. A spoilt one, a soppy one full of mawkishness. Given the times, anyone who holes up in there with bread and water guaranteed and a pure wool habit every year, doesn't she seem cunning to you? Eh? She doesn't even have to lift her skirt. Still, she's a brazen hussy; the lockup and the stench from the common grave serve her right. Yet she doesn't know what she's losing. Lifting and lowering my skirt, I'm more important here than she is. I can do anything. I'm the mistress of this pretty field. And she, what does she do? I'll tell you. She'll become blind, deaf, mad, will rot like a body without a shroud. She'll die like a dog."

The two women drift away. The Lombard goes into the second hut. Two tailors seated on a straw mat are cutting and sewing some black cloth; a painter kneels on the ground painting the suits just finished. Two young boys come and go, carrying pliers, hammers, bowls of plaster, and fresh water.

"Get out, you snoops, get out! Beat it, you idlers!" shouts a man coming in with a manikin under his arm.

The Lombard leaves and glimpses the Turnip in the distance, who repeatedly makes a sign to him, looking anxiously around. The Lombard goes to him. The Turnip, hidden behind the fountain, pulls him by the arm and softly asks him to kneel down next to him. "Be careful, the Gascon is looking for you. Blessed heaven, hide. He's in charge of the yards to the left and right of the church now. He directs everybody and decides everything. He's got a skewer this long he's taken from the sacristan's kitchen, the one he stabbed the Big Turk with. Yes, I know that. Surprised I'd tell you? My mouth's been dry since yesterday— I'm so scared I've got no saliva anymore, and my bones and my leg stumps are aching with fear.

"The Big Turk was a friend. Who'll protect me now? Who'll I beg with for alms? I'm afraid of staying here alone, and of having to go outside the cemetery walls. Someone like me—an apple core they call me—they'll kill me like nothing. If I had legs, I'd run away instead of hobbling here. But you, you can escape. The Gascon is looking for you. Here he is, Saint-Moor! It's him. Pretend nothing's happened, but don't forget what I told you."

With an agile move, the Turnip disappears behind the fountain. The Gascon passes close, without looking. He goes straight on silently, on the alert, as if he could see with his ears and shoulders. The Lombard, turning away, eludes him and disappears among the curious bypassers who are observing the preparations.

The Lombard then heads toward the big tent raised in the far corner, by the Arcade de la Lingères. Two mechanics and a carpenter work on a notched, wooden wheel connected to a spindle with a long, thick rope tied to it. When a lever is moved, a stake perpendicular to the ground lowers and rises. Standing in the middle of the tent is the man he'd seen the first day, the Moor Macabré, as the Big Turk had called him. He wears a long, lined, blue cape and boots wound with cloth bands. He attentively watches the work, drawing lines on a wooden tablet he holds in his hand and checking their length. From time to time he approaches the friar, also intent on tracing and measuring, and they discuss details in a low voice. They take turns consulting, then return to help the laborers working on a large wagon with a long bed, about twelve by thirty feet, covered with a black drape that hangs to the ground to hide the wheels. In the center of the wagon bed, soldered around a hole are thin, hammered leaves of copper alternating with strips of silvered fabric. Hidden underneath, three men try to work two enormous blacksmith's bellows. When the compressed air comes out of the hole, all the leaves move, shimmer, and vibrate with the robust sound of the fire. Lastly, at the far corner of the wagon bed two laborers work on a carcass made of wood that looks like the skeleton of a whale's head, and is fixed in such a way that moving it from below opens and closes its colossal, hideous mouth. Three little steps hide a passage that enables actors to ascend and descend unobserved from the wagon bed.

Maybe it's a premonition, thinks the Lombard. These heads, these preparations. Who stays? Who leaves? I or they? A strange feeling comes over me, another one of my obsessions, fixations of a too-tender heart, the Big Turk would have said. It occurs to me that I am a theater that is being prepared and all of them are pretending to be at work, but in reality they're spying on me, watching me. The inquisitive ones watching me are preparing themselves for a spectacle. And if I were bewitched? No, I'm just sick, sick in body, in mind. The Big Turk was right. But if he had had a permit ready now, the money for the toll, a bedroll, and a good overcoat as I do, wouldn't he have said, "I'm going." But where am I going, dammit, where?

Upright, silent, almost hidden in one of the octagonal tent's corners, the young Lombard is rapt in his thoughts, heedless to the coming and going of the workers and people snooping around. He is so immobile and has such a fixed stare that you'd say he's a manikin.

The Lombard thinks: I'll go, but tonight I'm too tired. Should I muster at the church of Saint-Jacques-la-Boucherie with the pilgrims getting ready to leave for Compostella? If I did stay here, what would change? Actually, a pilgrimage is a dubious undertaking. My grandparents were right. For them it was a sin, a dangerous illusion, to go far away looking for the truth in a dead body or the reliquary of an impostor.

Why then did I leave my home, the fields where I rode, my relatives, an occupation, friendly people, clean clothes, and porcelain pitchers. Why, just to end up here, where everything starts from scratch, suffocates, stinks. So different from what I was looking for. I wanted to see everything from one horizon to the other, over and under the mountains, along the rivers and beyond the valleys. In foreign countries. On long, adventurous voyages.

How many have seen, behind a frozen plateau, many thousands of miles from the Black Sea, the Caucasus valley of Tana?

That day at dawn we trudged over the snowy crossing, and down below, at the end of the trail we still had to traverse, there was a green valley you would have said is emerald. A sun-drenched valley, I thought, with strips of freshly plowed red earth and some villages—a mirage. Descending into the valley were orchards, and stone fortresses that no Christian merchant had ever seen. We stood there stunned to silence—was it perhaps Eden? It was the world. Here it was.

I had walked from Bari to Avignon; I left everything to become a virtual stranger, an alien. But now I'm tired, sick, bewitched. Because searching for the truth is one thing, but the black despair that seizes you afterward is something else. Doubt sniffs you out like a mangy dog. Then everything changes again. You think you understood; you understood it's all a game of which you're the only master. You tell yourself that all the tricks are finally only a way of playing the game. One day you're happy and the next you're desperate. But if I stay here, what will become of me? Here is a world of death. A strange place.

No, I'm sure of it. It's not by chance I came here. For a long while this Field espied me, pursued me, awaited me. Despite the journey's almost impossible conditions, I managed just the same to get here over the mountain heights, slipping through brigand territory, the grand duke's fiefdom, and the king's lands. Now I'm waiting for the reunion of the pilgrims that will be held at Saint-Jacques-la-Boucherie. Whoever arrives first at Mont Joyeux, from where you can see the cathedral in Compostella, will be called Le Roi, King of the long march.

Strange, but now I'm indifferent to all this.

When the Lombard leaves the tent, it is already dark,

evening. He drifts toward one of the arcades. It's cold, and the curious idlers have dispersed; here and there are bonfires. Under the arcade, the travelers and pilgrims huddle for warmth. The smell of bean soup is in the air. Someone has put a little piece of perfumed wood to burn on a torch. The Lombard lays his bedroll on the ground, sits down, pulls his hood up, folds his legs and stays like this.

An old man is telling the pilgrims about already having been twice to Compostella—Campo Stella, Field of the Star, to be exact. He talks about the stopping places on the road and puts them on guard against the journey's dangers. Marauders, he explains, pretend to be pilgrims. "They dress like you; they carry a pilgrim's staff, wear capes and thin chains. They mourn, recite litanies. But when you rest in an uninhabited place, a little behind the others, when you're alone on the road, they attack you, rob and kill you. The journey is long. Around Roncisvalle there is snow and there are wolves and soldiers. Stay always in a group, light night fires when you bivouac, and place your emblems in plain view. The wolves will flee and the others will leave you in peace. Some cities will open their doors to you and give you free bread; others will only send the militia to escort you to the borders of the fields. At Pamplona, all the bells will ring in celebration and you will be greeted like old friends. Some convents in the countryside will make you new sandals but, don't fool yourself, the way is long.

"At certain times, in certain valleys, you will be alone, exhausted, undefended. You will be sorry you undertook a trip like this. You will be assailed by doubt. It's then that the fake pilgrim will appear: He who pretends to be dying and, when you kneel to help him, will rob you and escape, by himself or with accomplices. He'll point you in another direction out of maliciousness or to make you hand over your goods. It's better, then, to have nothing, to start with little. Are you pilgrims or merchants? I've seen some leave with cash and bank drafts in order to buy merchandise to sell when they return. *Ignobilis mercatura.*

"I went twice and I will go again if these old legs will hold up, but let me tell you, as the proverb says, Whoever has ringworm shouldn't lift his cap. If you aren't sincere, don't go. As certainly as time flies, to claim you're sincere is like commanding the wind. Everything is topsy-turvy. On the road you will see camps destroyed or abandoned, peasants turned into bandits, brigands who became gentlemen, monasteries that are brothels, forsaken churches, thieving monks, and begging nobles. *Abyssus abyssum in vocat.* Even the poor are organized; watch out for charlatans who go to and fro in bands, always on the road between one city and another. They imitate priests, nuns, virgins, reliquary salesmen. They feign having Saint Vitus dance, Saint Moor's sickness; they wail, roll on the ground, drool piteously. But it's all fiction; there's always some man or pious woman to deceive."

The old man continues his story, pausing every now and then to answer questions, listing again all the places the pilgrims have to travel through: names of distant cities, forts and legendary abbeys.

It's terrible, the Lombard thinks to himself. And what if the old man were the first one to lie. My God, I've become suspicious! Just my way of feeling like an orphan again.

Someone has put some incense to burning right beside the

old pilgrim. A tired, embittered, old man, thinks the Lombard, watching him talk and cough in the midst of thick smoke plumes—a pagan god come back to exhort a cursed century.

A hand placed on his arm makes the Lombard suddenly turn. A man seated on the ground in front of him, leaning against a column, offers him a cup of soup. Maybe he sat down there while he was looking away; the Lombard tries to remember, but he is unable to say if that man was there when he entered the arcade. The Lombard shakes himself, takes the cup, and thanks the man.

"I have the look of being very hungry, eh?"

"No, friend, but you seem somewhat anxious; let's say, rather, obviously worried. But if you're afraid of dangers, why are you going?"

"I am worried. Yes, it's true," answers the Lombard, "but I'm not afraid of rogues, nor wolves, nor snow. It's knowing that going on the pilgrimage will be the same as staying here that bothers me so much. To travel with two thousand people you have to beware of hypocrisy, lust, revenge, swindles, always looking back over your shoulder, suspecting and imagining.

"Tell me, don't you think it's like living in the towns we decided to leave? All brothers on the journey, and all enemies. For me, this is sorry knowledge. Here it's like everywhere. But then why are all these people going away, if not to change? Or is it only for the secret dream of becoming King? For the fantasy of doing business? For adventure? That's what worries me. As the Big Turk said, a tenderhearted person like me is easily worried.

"But thanks, I was hungry, and this soup is good. What about you, tell me, are you, too, going to Compostella?"

The Lombard is seized by an intense euphoria.

Since he'd come to the cemetery, in trying to think of something he hadn't been able to pin down exactly, he was shadowed by a series of reflections. In his mind, he'd turned over again and again certain memories and facts about his life. He'd surrendered to a vague feeling, almost pleased to feel transported, ready to start over completely. If I'm here, he'd said to himself, in this typical fortified realm, it's because I've decided to recapitulate my entire life.

Still young, the Lombard had condensed the whole of his twenty-seven years of living into a full range of experience. The great mobility of his generation allowed him to travel, to learn much quickly, and to transform his experiences into a knowledge of life, thanks to some eclectic notions, some of which he'd inherited from his people, the Waldensian heretics of Piedmont. Other ideas of his century were in the air, such as the passion for alchemy and philosophical allegories. The Lombard found himself at the apex of a movement and at the intersection of the past and the future.

His people's tradition had given him a heritage of sympathy for popular protest; its heresy and biblical purism bore the spirit of reform. But the present, made up of mystical tensions and an adventurous impulse, tormented him, because the Lombard was a child of his time, a time of contrasts, of great ideas being born and of great ideas dying, and popular allegorical language, heavy with two-fold meaning, exalted and romanticized expectations. It was a ferocious time, whose world was unstable, and cruel. Yet people searched for harmony and a new humanity. It was a decadent world—pessimistic, irrational, corrupt; people were childish in the face of life, pompous and formalistic. At the same time the world was in innovative ferment.

The Lombard was right when he asked himself: Who was the Big Turk? And who is the walled-in woman? He'd intuited that they were like him in some way.

He'd gradually begun to reflect on all this after the first, almost primordial, contact with the special reality of the cemetery. But his thinking, by turns pertinent and prolix, again and again skipped over, deformed, ignored, invoked and idealized the facts. To pretend otherwise would be mistaken, because the Lombard was not a chance person from a distant century. Rather, he was the spirit of youth, vulnerable, ingenuous, yet tenacious, who ruminated with the relative means at his disposal. The Lombard was a man of 1424.

* * *

Yes, the Lombard is gripped by a strange euphoria. He's passed the day gloomily in the cemetery, alone once again after the Big Turk was killed. He's thought at length of that body thrown into the common grave. They said, "Yes, the Big Turk is dead." And no one thought anything of it. His bones will never lie with his father's and Famagosta will continue to exist without knowing that one of its citizens lies dead in this ground. But, in his thought the Big Turk was still with him: I mean here, some place in my head. And as long as I live, he lives, because here he has form and clarity. I can dream him, talk to him, and describe him. He exists as colors and images do. After all, as long as he exists in this way, it's a kind of life.

"No," says the man who had given him the cup of soup, "I'm not going to Santiago. I'm a pilgrim headed straight for Saint Peter's tomb."

The man who spoke has a long face, with something eccentric about it, as if the skin on his face were elastic. It is made of a series of long wrinkles and tucks. If he raises an eyelid, the purses beneath his eyes shift; if he smiles, his flabby cheeks slide toward his ears in a frank and at the same time mysterious and ironic expression. Then, suddenly, the face recomposes itself, turning serious again. But not for long. With each sentence, thought, and glance the crevasses on his face realign themselves into a series of new expressions so that there is always one side of his face that doesn't match the other—whether he's talking or not. The Lombard stares at him, fascinated and attentive. Here is somebody, he thinks, who by himself could mime a whole Mystery play.

His forehead is bald, but at the sides he has long, still dark, very fine hair, which sways like two synchronized curtains. All his clothes are dark gray, and he wears a cape and black boots.

"Let's say I'm a conscripted pilgrim, by order of the Council. As punishment, I have to make amends and go as far as Rome. Only when I come back will I have proved I completed my pilgrimage; and not until then will I be exonerated from my guilt—if guilt I have—and be given back my official papers and citizenship."

The man pauses, looks around carefully, and then continues speaking. The Lombard can't tear his eyes away from his face. "I come from Bohemia. Do you know where that is? More or less? It's a great distance and the trip is exhausting. But the first half is done. Upon arriving here, I bought a new pair of boots, and now I'm waiting for you pilgrims to depart to take advantage of the armed escort that will accompany you outside the walls, toward the south. I don't want to take too many chances. To die for a forced trek, let's say, is not for me. This journey doesn't interest me. I want to stay alive. I want to go back where I came from, to fight beside my people.

"Maybe I ought not have spoken to you like this. You could be a spy. Let me tell you, I've met plenty spies. Always ready to say, 'No, you aren't really repentant; you're a sinner forever.' They're always ready to accuse you and give your name to the Inquisition's secret agents. You're probably too young to even notice these things, but the spies, you know, are dispatched by the authorities. All kinds of them."

The man leans over a little more, as his low, slow voice has become almost a whisper. He leans back against the column and begins speaking again, looking deep into the Lombard's eyes. "I see that you talk in an elevated style. Excellent, excellent, they won't be able to understand us. Yes, those two, those seated down there. Note them well, two spies, two dogfaces. They would like to see me repentant, and they don't even know for what. They don't know how to think; they don't know how to discriminate. They only know how to bay. Someone told them to mix among the pilgrims, to observe those who are working off punishments ordered by the council, to listen and track down heretics. Listen to subversives' conversations, to the proud and unrepentant. But I have no fear; my journey's still not finished. I'm a penitent who has to say he is. I, repentant? I will say 'Yes.'"

The Bohemian pauses again. The Lombard, no longer able to contain his curiosity, asks him in an urgent, low voice what he was to repent for.

"There was a man who came, challenged everyone, and talked about how things really stood. They charged him, and the Council condemned him to be burned at the stake. I listened to his speeches. I'm a notary, and I'm Bohemian. I know my people. I know that to live in freedom is important. I can tell you that if people hadn't begun to fight, no one would have freed them from slavery, ever. And because what he said was right, people rebelled, freed the lands, and organized their own militias. That's why I took to listening to that man's speeches.

"Maybe in another situation all this wouldn't have happened. But there are some moments in the summer when the hot wind courses and, with the wind, the fire. That's the way it was then, a splendid summer. How come? You haven't heard about these things? You don't know that the Bohemians are fighting against Emperor Sigismund, the Roman Church, and the Goths? That's why the Council of Constance sent John Hus, the Master of Husinec, to the stake. Let's say, rather, that he was lured into a trap, betrayed, and assassinated like a bandit. But if you don't know, it's useless for me to tell you. What can these things mean to you! And don't make me say what I ought not."

The Lombard is anxious to hear more about these extraordinary events, and he pleads with the Bohemian to go on. "Really," he says, "it's precisely because I don't know that you have to tell me. Don't reveal secrets, just tell me what happened."

The Bohemian nods. "All right. I'm still not at Rome, after all, so I can still speak. Maybe these events will be important to you. There's something in your eyes. Let's say I think you're sincere. I'll try to tell everything in a few words.

"The Council and the ecclesiastical tribunal accused everybody of heresy, Bohemians and the Master's disciples. I too am a sympathizing heretic. But it's a question of two things: For them it's supporting an emperor—who oppresses us—but for us it's openly proclaiming a religion accepted by free people. Is a person who wants justice a heretic?

"So, there's a war now in Bohemia. The people managed to retake a lot of land from the proprietors, the bishops, and the Emperor, lands that were governed by others—mercenaries, soldiers, and foreign nobility. A long war, years. But the people won and our nation, Bohemia, was born.

"The people haven't forgotten the Master, nor the great Jerome. Who's he? How could you not know him? The Roman Church always arranges things; when it bans people, it brands them outlaws.

"But after the Emperor's troops threw thousands of Bohemians into the old mine holes, who can doubt who the real Antichrist is? And so I'm not penitent. I still don't repent, let's say. For me to repent—though in the end I'll have to—it will take many stops on my trip and some long months of reflection on the way to Rome. I still have to think about this and many other things.

"You know that the Master's followers have taken a mountain and called it Tabor, like Mount Tabor near Nazareth where the transfiguration occurred? There are no servants or masters there. They said, 'We'll share everything justly and equally, make things right, keep everything in common.' Is it possible? I don't know. The road is long, and I'll have time to understand better and to learn. News reaches even here, brought by pilgrims, and everywhere you meet heretics who escape and hide, Meanwhile, I say, all right, you want me to repent? But my repenting doesn't mean repenting on account of them. What difference does my repenting or not repenting matter if things are as they are?"

The Lombard nods assent. "It's true, one can't repent for a whole population. The fact is that when things begin to change, you can't ignore them. I've listened carefully to what you've told me, and it interests me very much. I like it. Facts are sad, but these new facts aren't common; they could change the world. I like that. Now I understand why you want to go back."

"If I'm not assassinated in an ambush and if I manage to return, it will be a sign. Friend, for a notary to be banished, without citizenship, and condemned to be a perpetual pilgrim is destiny's joke." The Bohemian closes his eyes. "Enough of these stories. Tell me, who is the Big Turk?"

This catches the Lombard by surprise. "You too know him? How?"

"You mentioned his name just a while ago, and a notary has a good memory. I would like to know who can have such an unusual name. Let's say, even, that I'd like to change the subject."

The Lombard feels confused. There were still so many things that he would like to ask in order to know more about the events of which the Bohemian spoke. He knows it won't be easy to sum up the Big Turk in a few words. "Well, actually the subject won't be so different," he declares decisively. "The Big Turk, too, was a conscripted pilgrim." The Lombard wants to give a definitive answer. "In life he was like a boat that ran aground on a menacing pack of seaweed. He was someone who went on his way with a fine stride because he'd never forgotten odors. His stubborn boat, forced to wend through this cemetery, foundered a little, but from the height of the mainmast he settled on the right direction. And he was generous and considerate of people, including a group of mendicants who were his companions. He also wanted, in his way, to change the world. But he had enemies who laid a trap for him. The Gascon stabbed him last night with a skewer.

"Do you want to know more? All this may seem odd to you, and in fact, it is a strange story. These facts, even if of minor importance compared to those you've told me, are still similar to the consuming fire of your summer."

"But why was the Big Turk killed?" asks the Bohemian, turning softly on his side.

"Why?" exclaims the Lombard. "Yes, why indeed! My God, you're a logical, rational man. You immediately draw a clear, concise line between things. Look, I haven't asked myself even now why he was killed—a half-crippled beggar, son of a Turkish woman and a Genovese ex-seaman and customs worker. The Big Turk ended up here without a travel permit. Why did he have to be assassinated? Look, I don't know. I really can't tell you why. Maybe the answer isn't a concrete reason but an entity, a being called the Gascon—another beggar, but a cunning one, whose maliciousness made him want to annihilate the Big Turk. Now that I think of it, maybe there is a reason, a secret one I don't know."

The Bohemian is absolutely still, staring at him, searching his face as if he wants to learn something more. Then suddenly he changes the subject and asks him, "But you, how did you get here?"

"I? One day I left my house with some merchants to see the world, and then, after having traveled a great deal, working for the merchants in the name of someone else became unbearable. So, I decided to take to the road by myself. If I find a teacher, I told myself, I'm going back to my land and start all over. To begin reading again after having seen what the world's like is more important than studying without ever having seen anything. To read without having seen anything makes you the slave of all those gentlemen in the university. All of them are great hypocrites who bungle, copy, and steal to impress students and others. Do you know how many chamois gloves the candidate must give to the teachers even before enrolling in order to get a diploma? At Novara, twelve. And there's all the rest: despite the sacrifices, when you go to their courses they make you feel like a worm. I was ashamed of my peasant grandparents with their odd habits. I was timid. Damn.

"But one day I was no longer impressed. Listening to talk of philosophy from other, different people, I was interested in being better acquainted with it and in studying alchemy texts. But I didn't have the means, and, although I thought I understood their words, in reality I didn't understand at all. I was impatient, in a hurry. And so one day I left. I thought the first thing to do was to search for the truth, or anything you call by that name.

"Leaving wasn't difficult, because in my part of the country there are lots of merchants. So, I went with a rich man from Brescia to Genova, where I stayed for about two years. Maybe I crossed paths there with the Big Turk's old father. You, who like finding connections between things, can you explain to me all these threads strung between humans' destinies?

"From Genova I embarked as a clerk on ships that carry goods to Turkey and the Black Sea. I stayed in those places four years and that's why I learned the Turkish language. I went as far as the Orient, beyond the Tana Valley, toward India.

"Before the war, the Genovese came there regularly. There was a place—I no longer remember what it's called—but the customs was located there. There were people in the markets from every nation—Armenians, Turks, Arabs, Indians, Tartars. For me traveling was a swim around the world. Now you're taken by the obsession of returning to your own people, but back then I was seized by an opposite madness: I wanted to go away from them, far away. That's probably because I was orphaned very young, so I looked for a boundless, general family. Then I understood, we're a family, yes, but with the defects of all large families—fights, abuses, and hierarchies.

"I needed to become a loner again. And I told myself, now's the time to leave everything and start over. But, I wondered, a pilgrim? A Waldensian pilgrim? Still, even if my grandparents prohibited pilgrimages, I thought I had to make one, all alone. Not a journey to a reliquary or an impostor saint, but a journey to experience purification. I told myself, if everything goes well, I'll then go back to my homeland and devote myself to work.

"Have you ever seen an initiate this inert for so many years? You know what I'm saying? If I'm not mistaken, you're a philosopher."

The Bohemian gives him a half-serious look. "I, a philosopher? Don't joke. But let's say I know what you're talking about.

In Bohemia they hold great discourses about these things. Be careful, however; lower your voice."

"I know. I shouldn't go around talking about my Waldensian grandparents and alchemy. There's an edict from the king and a Papal Bull from Pope Jean that accuses alchemists of being like heretics, according to which I, by their logic, would be doubly heretical and unfaithful. But my papers are all in order and I'm ready for the great gathering of pilgrims. I said to myself: If I choose Compostella it's not by chance; and, in fact, you know everybody's going there, the sincere and the impostors, with the secret hope of finding marvelous things, of discovering the secret of transmutation.

"When I was traveling in the East, I met a mathematician who told me not to hurry. Everything takes its time to ripen, and in the human soul everything *happens*. But here, people have lost their heads, rushing and searching greedily. Damn. Who has the time to wait anymore? With the war and the uncertainties between birth and death everybody looks for gold. And maybe things are going so badly because of so much greed. *Who* wants to transmute *what?* Look, I liked what you told me a little while ago. Because when a lot of people stick together and hold to an idea, if the idea has the necessary ingredients, things change. This world is a great furnace of combustions.

"I'll tell you something I've been thinking about since yesterday: In his patched clothes, the Big Turk kept a folded rag where he hid a pinch of rough salt. It wasn't magic dust, nor a crushed reliquary, and not even the grass they eat in the Holy Land. It really was salt, which I put in his mouth when he was dying. But, in his mind he could transmute this salt into other things, and who knows into what sensations and feelings that he didn't have time to tell me about. I guarantee you, when he smelled his salt I saw his expression change, even if it was dark. And from some of his words and the deep calm of his body I knew he was happy.

"I thought, how could this be? After all, this man is not educated, not a teacher, not a believer. Well, I said to myself, the truth is that the Big Turk was a body totally transmuting. His cause was just; his art was his way of philosophizing, even if he never forgot to eat his chickpeas, and then to belch. I don't know, I would say that he discovered the soul. This is what I was thinking about earlier."

Almost all the torches are out. The Lombard closes his eyes. He would like to keep on talking, but doesn't know where to start. There are so many things he wants to say. He is afraid of boring the Bohemian, who seems absorbed in other thoughts. He is surprised to hear the Bohemian ask, "And the salt?"

"The salt," the Lombard answers, "certainly. The Big Turk not only transformed his mind; he also knew how to transmute some of this world's matter into a noble, unearthly thing. He produced his gold."

The Bohemian interrupts him, "Ah! Then it was really salt; that's what the Big Turk hid."

The Lombard is surprised. He doesn't understand why the Bohemian, laughing with his eyes shut tight, is reacting this way now to what he had told him earlier. The Bohemian's unpredictable behavior, remarks initiated and interrupted, his way of laughing makes him uneasy. How is it possible, thinks the Lombard, that this man, so composed and knowledgeable, who has recounted such extraordinary events, marvels now at a fact, unusual, yes, but irrelevant to him.

The Bohemian laughs soundlessly. Only his hair moves, as if tossed by a vehement storm. He looks into the distance, inspecting the churchyard lying in darkness, then in a dry, precise voice whispers, "Young man, what you've told me is important. Your beggar companion had extracted gold from salt, but the Gascon you talked about, with his greed will have only salt for gold. In his mouth there will be a bitter taste."

"Really, I don't quite understand what you're saying," answers the Lombard.

"You will understand, you will. I assure you. If you don't understand on your own, tomorrow I'll explain what I meant to say. I'm tired, and it's already late—everybody's sleeping. It's better for us to sleep, too, and not talk. We'll wake up at dawn. Tomorrow the most famous spectacle in the history of the city begins, made especially for these exalted people. As if there weren't already a great spectacle in this cemetery, thousands of them in fact—and each one astonishing."

The Bohemian pulls his cowl over his head, readjusts the cape on his shoulders, lays his head on his bed sack covered with red fabric and, looking at the Lombard, gestures goodnight. But the Lombard notices a strange expression on his face, as if under the folded cowl the Bohemian is still laughing to himself in the silence of his body, laughing happily about something the Lombard can't understand. But what? he thinks, and feels alone again.

6

ALIX'S SECOND SOLILOQUY

I CAN SAY THAT for a while I lived in memory. No, not on or from memory, but in memory, in a memory of having lived. As if my body went forward on its own, knowing what to do and what not to do.

A life had ended and I had a respite; I did my novitiate. I did my duty absent-mindedly, without attention or feeling. It really didn't interest me. My emotions were so strong, absolute, and decisive that this experience seemed like a parody to me. Forced to enter a convent, I thought the monotonous, false life, packed with stupidities, resembled my mother's merchant husband. To revolt against this imposture meant revolting against him. A huge mercantile business is what finally counted in life for him. Each "I give you" was a "you give me," each request an entry on the books, a sum, a calculation of cycles somehow infinite.

I didn't revolt openly. But deep down for some time I had already revolted in a sequence of tiny, irreversible steps. I wanted to let my conscience decide in everything and for everything, the sole rhythm of it being dictated by my inner time. I still didn't feel strong; I needed to feign. For me it was a matter of saying "yes," or saying "no," doing this or doing that, trying to hide my withdrawal, and maintaining intact within me a domain I didn't want to nor could reveal. I wouldn't, however, have known how to describe this domain. How would an outsider have been able to understand?

I rarely spoke during my novitiate; my lack of enthusiasm was obvious. I had taken so much time to achieve a certain mastery of myself that now I could dissemble, and yet didn't want to. I knew how to feign a conscientious performance of my apprenticeship, but I didn't want to make-believe too much. I did not want to display those childish and exaggerated sentiments that I saw so often during my novitiate.

Since I tolerated the novice's experiences, and since I was more capable of reading the texts, calculating, and speaking, I was protected by the Sister Superior. However, they never understood why I would do my work and the required prayers, but as soon as we were allowed to amuse ourselves, instead of participating in all those customary activities that seemed unendurable to me, I isolated myself.

Our order was corrupted by fashionable ceremonies and superstitious beliefs. I couldn't bear what was said about the soul and about everything that I felt expanding in my body. Yes, I was strange. I invented secret names that enabled me to think my thoughts untainted. The foolish conversations of the novices, the occasional preaching of the prioress, and the monks' admonishments made me shiver, provoked a kind of physical irritation that made my muscles grow rigid.

Once a religious representative of the grand duke's came— small, ugly, and mean—who kept us with a long sermon filled with citations of ancient allegories in order to reach a conclusion: a pronounced disdain for us young women. He had composed it by taking some citations from the Golden Legend, Peter of Lombard, Anselm, everybody. But not knowing how to read, he learned everything by memory and ended up totally confused.

In that awfully long year, I sometimes found myself confronting lascivious old men who were either fake friars or ignorant canons who treated the novices with vulgarity and condescension. Our situation as women consecrated to chastity—for good or ill—made these men sour and suspicious. I couldn't stand how they indulged themselves in talking to me about eternity. What could it have meant to me if I was given an indulgence of seven quarantines when time seemed incalculable?

Earlier, when I was living in the Saint-Eustache quarter, I had heard some mendicants' or vagabond preachers' public sermons in a convent courtyard or in the market square. They were often unscheduled, without a permit from the seneschal or the archdeacon, and so the preachers were regularly thrown out by the guards, after which there were violent scuffles between the public and the soldiers because people wanted to hear them. They never tired of listening to the sermons, which were clear and direct.

Once a Dominican called Vincent stayed three days and three nights, barricaded in the Jacobins' convent, protected by women and poor people who threw hot ashes, stones, and urine down on the soldiers. There were always unofficial preachers on whom the authorities looked askance. When a belief is felt, it's held out of conviction, out of passion, and not for the sake of form or out of habit.

At the convent only those who were accredited by the canon or the prioress came to preach. Other preachers were at work everywhere in the country to exhort the people. With the long war and the imminent arrival of the English, who had time to

pay us any attention? Besides, we had to work in the public re-
fectories and help in the hospitals.

The situation among the novices was not much different
from that of the rest of the people. Some of the girls were from
the nobility who believed they were superior to the common-
ers, and so on down to the poorest who performed the hardest
and most miserable work. Many were still attached to the fashionable and courtly life, received visits, and, being excused
from some regulations, went out to receptions. Others, alternating between outbursts of good will and obsession with sin, accepted conventional arrangements of indulgences and prayers
without trying to understand what they were doing there in the
convent.

I never talked about what I felt. For others in the convent, my
words would have been like a clangor that would have fractured
all their worlds of reflected, opaque, and illusory images. I was
exactly like them—I felt neither superior nor inferior—but I felt
a thousand miles away, in another place. In any case, they
wouldn't have understood. Even I still didn't understand really
what had happened, how I'd been transported from the magic
world of my childhood onto this course. And since I talked to
Him continually, and at certain moments that seemed special,
or when I was alone and said *my* prayer without being watched,
it was difficult to pretend to encounter Him only during matins.
Those identical morning prayers, uttered in a monotone and
from memory in a sustained whisper that put goodness on show
as proof of piety, seemed absurd to me.

But I said nothing. Maybe I was afraid they might accuse me
of heresy, witchcraft, or something similar. Yes, of course. A per-

son was accused of heresy by one of the popes just because he claimed that his Lord had practiced absolute poverty. That year there had been countless pyres and the Inquisition's secret agents had infiltrated even the convents.

So I wasn't ashamed of having dissembled. It was a way of keeping myself inviolate. No, I was not a deceiver, but honest. It was a way of keeping apart. I felt dissimilar and was afraid. Now on my own, I was still more vulnerable, for by this time I was an orphan, without funds, without friends or protectors. My mother had had a son during the last year of my novitiate and had disinherited me.

From that time on, no one looked for Alix. I had become Agnes, my new name as a novitiate.

* * *

The first year dragged on forever. I seldom saw the city or my favorite places. When I did it was on the run; I was never alone, always escorted. I could no longer spend the whole day walking about the streets along with the inhabitants of my quarter, all the way to the city walls as I had so much enjoyed doing.

Because of battles lost and the growing misery, the situation worsened. They talked of new plagues they said had decimated the population in the southeastern part of France, and they knew the English would not be deterred. Entire convents from that region were reduced to begging. Our way of life had become one more of labor than prayer. The majority of the girls who weren't of the nobility were sent out to the numerous processions and funerals that took place almost every day, and the poorest went to the hospitals and the public eating places to work when they weren't serving the needs of the convent itself.

The result of all this outside disorder was that I less easily hid my intolerance. Lacking the rigid discipline to assume the guise of daily deeds, I lost contact with things.

I seemed to lose a sense of time.

I thought of what the Dominican friar had told me about the theory of a heretic philosopher who viewed life as a sequence of realms inhabited by ideas and transcendent souls. Realms, he said. Were they spread out over the earth and sky? I imagined them, instead, as a vertical stairway in the mind and in nature, with a lesser density of matter at the top and a greater density at the bottom. My tutor would never allow me to reflect on this subject.

"A girl? Theology? No! Impossible," he shouted and nervously closed his drooling mouth. I don't know how the conversation about angels' sex ended, but I perceived that my tutor was quite sure that he knew very well what the devils' sex was. As if "being" were not first of all a transcendental emanation. As to women theologians, what would he have said to the great Catherine when she wrote directly to Pope Gregoire in her name and of Jesus crucified?

It wasn't true that I was possessed as my mother thought, nor was I a poor soul incapable of understanding life. I felt life as if it were a concrete reality and did not underestimate its importance. Even before my father died, I had wanted to confront it and I had no intention of fleeing from it, even if it was frightening. It was my relation to life, and with something else that I never managed to define, but which could be called non-life instead of death, that tormented me. I dwelt untiringly on both of them in the convent and always bore them willingly.

The second year I wanted to do my part with the nurses who devoted themselves to duties at the Hotel-Dieux on the island. I went for a whole night, until dawn, three times a week to look after the ill. No, I didn't cure them, I was only an inexpert novice, but I helped clean and wash their sores and ulcers with warm water, put on bandages, and gave them drinking water. I also swept and mopped. There was a great deal of work; it seemed there was no end to the wounded, sick, and dying. Everywhere the hospices and charitable institutions were full of people who came from far away—refugees from war, pilgrims, and abandoned women, as well as bands of children no one looked after any more.

Although my body was ever-present, I had the strange feeling back then that life and I no longer shared bounds. It's as if we were out of phase, one of us always either a second ahead or behind the other, each in its own orbit. You were there, a little behind me, suspended and luminous. I say, "You," yes, because I'm no longer in the habit of talking to anyone, that is, of simply talking, of making sounds. Actually, I'm trying to talk about a Thing. Or, rather, about the being of a Thing, about its mysterious, feminine emanation.

I wanted to be acquainted with "You"—without getting credit; I didn't want anyone to say, "Oh, look, Agnes is on the way." The relation had to be unambiguously without recompense. The only reward I chose for this life was this secret intimacy. So, naturally they said, "Agnes is strange; she doesn't talk to Him like the others do. She'll probably be good only for bookkeeping, a clever abbess."

But I already knew that I wasn't made to be a novice, a sister, a prioress, or to be a saint or exalted reformer, but only to be a messenger, the bearer of a strange presence: I was inhabited by the Thing. Perhaps they'll say I'm obsessed. No, not demonic, as they could say, but the iridescence of a distant sunrise. Nothing more than a witness.

I had investigated life quickly, taken it in hand like a crystal alembic, and had discovered myself infinitely extended by this embrace of deliverance. I knew this saved me from organic death. Only time was needed to show me how, I thought.

*　*　*

And so the second year came around, still more confused and unsettling. The young king had fled the city when it was retaken by the grand duke; the war went on with its massacres and contradictory reports. The people no longer dared think how long it would go on—fifty, a hundred years. Counting would do no good, and waiting was frightening. It only made people vainly ask themselves: But when will the end come?

Down at the hospital on the island, every time the bell rang the sick intoned a long litany of laments out of fear of the invader. But no one knew any longer with which invader they would finally have to deal. The city had been taken and retaken in those years by so many parties and had been stricken by so many catastrophes that in the end the people beheld the English as they did the others; they alternately hated or strangely anticipated them.

At present the English are masters of the city. The day they came, the sacristan brought the pitcher of water to my church-yard cell late in the evening after vespers; he stood on the stool, fidgeting, grousing. They came in May, the month when the Big Turk used to bring me garlands, the month I used to walk in the hills.

They came like all attackers. From my cell I heard the kindled noise of the city: the sound of arms, bells, shouts. During long silences I thought the city had let itself be occupied. It was not defeated, just conquered. Then all the nobility and high offi-cials came to the solemn mass with the regent Lancaster.

My second novitiate year ended some months before the re-turn of the grand duke and many years, five, I think, before the English came. That year something happened that I took as a sign, one that I was waiting for. The time was ripe for my life to change.

One day by a fortunate accident I accompanied a superior, Sister Mercedes, who had been urgently called to the bedside of a dying relative in the Saint-Paul quarter. We were as far as Saint-Georges when I made the final and definitive decision.

Sister Mercedes had a deeply noble and discrete soul that gilded everything with a touch of grace. When she talked, she made life simple and clear. It was a pleasure for me to accom-pany her, even if her conversation at times gave me a vague feeling of discomfort and even if her clarity magnified my own troubled state. But that day she didn't talk, and I, abstracted, looked around me as we were walking. That day more than ever I felt completely present and awake—in fact, alive!—but also disabled, paralyzed by that very reality. As if, paradoxically, I was due still to awaken, although being, as I said, awake. Or, perhaps, the reality around me, existing in equivocal time, took on a mirrored life beyond which there was another reality, and still another.

I was thinking about all of this, trying to order my feelings logically, when we arrived. Sister Mercedes told me then that she was going to stay there because she probably would have to be awake the entire night and that, seeing that it was still early, it wasn't necessary for me to remain. She gave me permission to leave and return to the chapel; I would have to retrace the way by myself. After all, I wasn't going far and there was still daylight.

Coming out, I took a turn around the large grassy square in front of the church. In that part of the open space where it widened and ran to the river, there was a huge crowd. There weren't just the usual river fishermen, vegetable peddlers, and laborers waiting for daily work. No, there were many more people than usual. Many, too many. It seemed like an enormous spectacle. I had forgotten that it was one of the favored places for executions. Because I came from behind the church, I found myself close to the soldiers that were holding him. I never learned who he was nor of what he was guilty. Maybe he's a knight, I thought.

The confusion was manifold. There were guards with massive horses. I stopped to look; for the first time in my life I felt curious about an execution. Had I by chance gotten a craving like all the curiosity seekers who'd gathered for this event? I told myself: It's better that you leave immediately. But I couldn't. Not being far from him, I could see him clearly. He stood motionless, head down, motionless, absolutely motionless. He knelt slightly only when the confessor approached him. His gestures were maybe a little stiff, but he didn't tremble nor did he cry out. I was drawn by this control and I went still closer, conscious of my act, until I found myself almost directly in front of him.

I had forgotten what a man was. Seeing so many ignorant abbots, so many raving, preening, gawking people, I had truly forgotten. That man wore simple, black, close-fitting trousers and a shirt of fine, white fabric. Nothing else. Although he wore no other garments, I kept thinking he might be a knight. His smooth hair was pulled back into a knot, just a simple knot. Staring at him, I wondered what he might have done to be executed without the sign of his rank. Certain nobles sometimes wanted to die dressed for the ceremony and some notables wanted their insignias and the toga. Surely that white, clean shirt didn't mark him as a prisoner, that subtle and human face couldn't be that of a sorcerer or forger. He seemed to have no relative or friend in the crowd, no one who wept or supplicated the guards. Absolutely no one.

The guards went about their business preparing for the execution, and I thought I had better go away. Then he looked around. His gaze, how to say it? It seemed in an instant to have congealed this whole century. It immobilized the onlookers around him, showing them that his guilt was unfounded, accused them of bestiality, and then soared above them to an unendurable dimension, a dimension no longer human.

He was like one who let himself be possessed by devils only in order to deceive them, but, in reality, he was no longer there. He was already gone; he was inviolable. He had taken the measure of the spectators and left them for dead forever in the brace of an instant, while they, unconscious, stood there before him open mouthed and howling, ferocious and impatient.

Damnation!

They had understood nothing. How are these barriers possible? I thought. I felt paralyzed. I wanted to throw myself between them, to make clear what was not understood. A man, a body, a sacred Thing—but those blinded, crazed wolves, always ravenous, were rooted there. What could be done to awaken them?

Or was it true what I used to think as a girl? That their realm is this very world of opaque matter that dominates them and blinds them even more.

When he saw me, he stared at me. He went to the depths, through the black holes of my eyes, straight to the marrow. He communicated to me in a place where we exist outside of time.

Behind him was the Thing. That's when I understood that it exists in a space completely different from ours. Our space, so sky-struck, sometimes so sunny and so full of nature, is only the content of an enormous funnel, a womb. In an instant I saw beyond it, I saw the true space. Beyond, all around.

But not around our body, not in our air and our sky, but outside, beyond a membrane that encloses our bodies, our air, and our very sky. What we think of as outside had suddenly become an "inside," minuscule and relative. The true beyond, the true far off, is immense, vast, spacious, absolutely different in its dimensions, yet extremely close to me. It came to me from within a body, from that man's eyes. Something that I seemed to intuit so clearly in an instant had mysteriously connected a limitless space to an impalpable spark inside my body.

For a long time after this, when I was already in the church-yard cell, I continued thinking that that man had deposited his life in me, that he had taken flight through my body, as when one launches a bark in a river that flows to an unsuspected place.

Then they grabbed him and tied him, each limb to a horse. The crowd approached and retreated like a pulsing organ. People's eyes squinted; their mouths were agape. In all truth, that man was the calmest. Once more we stared at each other. Then I left. I felt crushed, and edged away, unable to control myself any longer.

Every movement felt immediate, next to my arm, my foot, my other arm, other foot—the preparations, the people ha-ranguing with coarse breath through decayed teeth, their screaming. The soldier mounting his horse: one, two, three, four horses. The drum roll, the confessor's prayer, the horses' restiveness, the mob slinking closer, more tense; body odors, hidden stenches under rags, tunics, skirts.

One, two, three, four. And I heard a sound unlike any other, a sound of joints being torn asunder and bones ripped away from each other.

Then I knew that that man had been dismembered, decapi-tated, tortured and that every part of his body was exposed at a city gate. When they told me I thought, well, so I'll never go again to Porte Saint-Martin, or to the gardens, or in any other place because even the pebbles conspire with this world of evil.

Then I vomited against the wall.

I had so little in my stomach that only some liquid came out.

I was seized with convulsions. After that I don't exactly know what happened, because I took to walking here and there; I had to have walked for a long time. How I paid the toll on the bridge I don't know. I no longer have any memory of it.

I came to a place that seemed unfamiliar to me, because the ground was covered with fresh grass and brimming with flowers. It was only for the festive arrival of one of the princesses, but in my delirium I took that quarter for another world. I needed to see fresh, natural, green things.

My thirst was terrible, and I would have drunk with my feet, my hands, stomach. My whole body thirsted with a bitter taste, a widespread, dry heat, like a ball of heat without flames. I had a fever. I walked like this until evening. When they found me, I had lost consciousness in the Carmelite cloister. The chaplain recognized me and made me spend the night in one of the chapels watched over by the sacristan's wife. They thought I was dying and lighted all the candles and incense.

At sunrise I awoke. The prioress of my convent was there. She had been accompanied by a very pale Sister Mercedes, who had spent the night with a dying person and had come here to look after another.

But, no, I wasn't dying; I lived.

The prioress went with me again. Would she have me punished? Tried for my eccentricity? My decision was already made: I would be a recluse.

So I spent three months isolated. They let me reflect. Besides having to talk to the canon and having my request acknowledged by the bishop, I had to reflect further and talk with those in charge of our diocese. Sister Mercedes and the prioress didn't really understand this decision, and secretly hoped that I might change my mind.

I wasn't punished nor was I suspected of being demonized. The confessor absolved me and no one thought of me as "that witless one;" rather, everyone said, "That's Agnes!" However, I had decided. Suddenly things began to come together clearly. I could not crack life from without. A girl—a strange young woman who had nothing—I could subdue reality only by turning it inside out.

I spent three serene, eventless months, three long summer months looking out a window at a corner of the cloister, at some trees. Summer had always had a magic effect on me; it's a time for increase and wonder. By then I had been able to convince everyone of my decision. I had even gotten the young king's permission.

What was I if not an orphan, a public object without a future, a young woman who couldn't make any decision without the endorsement and agreement of superiors? But the king didn't know then that a little later he would have to flee hurriedly and hide when the city was retaken by the grand duke—and that I, instead, would remain here in this churchyard cell for the rest of my life.

He had thought that I would likely be secluded in a parish monastery, in a calm, remote spot.

"Have you chosen a secure place in the country to the west?" the prioress asked me.

"No," I said, "I want to be enclosed in the outside wall of the church of the Cemetery of the Holy Innocents."

She was surprised, certainly. She muttered only some confused remarks. And I thought: Isn't it there, perhaps, the entryway to the great funnel, the opening into the Thing, the hermetic tomb and ground of all? No, I didn't say exactly this. I said something more general. But I was firm in my decision.

"A profound act of devotion," they called it—the prioress and everyone who was interested in my case. How else could they interpret my decision? I wasn't insane; whoever came in contact with me spoke of being convinced of my sincerity. I was calm, prepared. I lived in a luminous, impalpable dimension. I was prepared to leave for a transformed space.

In those isolated months before my reclusion, the prioress and Sister Mercedes often came to see me and bring me something to drink and eat, and to amuse me with the most recent news. So, until the last, I continued to follow the city's events.

The grand duke had retaken the city. Exasperated by the taxes imposed by the king, by the forced recruitment that squandered so many men in a war without end, by the surveillance of guards and spies found everywhere—even at public marriages and simple family reunions—the people opened their doors to him just as before they had opened them to the opposing party, and to the grand duke even earlier when he had won the first time. The truth is that the people kept hoping.

But a power that had just entered the city, that treated the people like animals, that incited them to massacre, to butcher others who like them were victims of earlier insanities, and then left them heaped in the streets like dirty pigs, what war could it win? The party of the Bludgeon, the party of the Carpenter's Plane, the parties of the king or the grand duke, will never solve anything if they don't change everything, truly everything.

To change, to transform: So easy to say, but in reality so difficult to do. That's the thing. Certainly, watching the Big Turk
wandering through the arcades from my hiding place, listening
occasionally to his verses, I understood that each one has his
decision to make in life and his way of accomplishing the
change—I have mine, you yours. To change within and without—not easy. Which standard should we take to guide us,
which ideal, which idea? How can one be sure about how and
what to change? And then I would say to myself, it's useless to
make this search so complicated.

The soul, that's it.

The soul expands in you, in the Big Turk, in the executed
man, in whomever has felt the urgent need for something other
than this heavy, opaque matter. Their need, their aspiration reflect the unifying movement toward the place where everything is clear and ideas are native.

The prioress and Sister Mercedes used to visit me and tell me
about the latest events. Even now, Sister Mercedes occasionally
comes to pray in front of my cell, and I, for my part, repeat the
words and pray with her. It seems the prioress has died. When
Sister Mercedes talks to me through my cell's narrow window I
don't always understand well, and since I don't want her to see
me, I stand aside, resting my head against the wall. At first I let
her see me, and stood diagonally from the fissure, but then, to
avoid the curious, I warned her that I would no longer let myself be seen but that I would pray with her.

Every time there's a festival here or an important funeral, or
an annual ceremony, the inquisitive come to the cemetery and
many of them stop under my cell. Some would like to see me

only out of curiosity; others carry candles and make vows, prayers, promises. Some simply insult me. But I never respond. The sacristan knows that I don't like this behavior, because I'm neither a saint nor a witch nor an omen. I can't make miracles. To respond would invite misunderstanding, encourage people to delude themselves with an image that is useful only for expressing their devotion.

One day I understood that I would never again have to be seen. If I were to show myself, I'd have to do it for everyone. What would it mean then to be a recluse? I would become an authority, a profession. So I stay back; I follow a rhythm known only in the churchyard. My outside contacts channel through the sacristan who brings me bread and a pitcher of water at sunrise. He always manages to speak and mutter something, some pieces of news he thinks might interest me. Every once in a while I look out, but only in the evening and when no one can see my eyes through the opening. When I look I cover myself with my tunic.

Sometimes I get to talking, like now, but it's almost impossible to hear me. My voice frightens me; it seems to issue from a distant place. Perhaps I don't talk, only whisper. These walls echo murmurs.

But don't think I don't know what's happening, that I don't follow the coming and going of groups, ladies, funerals. I recognize the voice of the old woman, the one who was already here when I came to sit under the Arcade de la Vierge. I'm familiar also with the slow, shambling step of the gravedigger. I grasp strands of conversations, the beggars' singsong, the rows and the calls of soup vendors. From the smell, I know if the common grave is full or if it was emptied. I can hear the gravedigger's wheelbarrow coming and going, up and down, discarding fleshless bones. What they say is true: This earth is powerful. It's a fertile soil that reduces the body to bones in only nine days.

There are so many other things I can hear! You become attentive, alert to noises—habits, voices, cracking stones. I heed time. I know when certain migratory birds fly over, and when pilgrims tend to gather.

Yes, I wanted to see the world this way, anchored, and from a crevice. But not just any world, no, but rather this model world in which everything happens. I wanted to abolish movement because even it is a contamination, a way of yoking yourself to dead matter. At least, it's this way for me as one who's chosen to disdain matter. Because abolishing movement at a certain, precise moment in life, and by your own will, is quite different from imprisonment and forced reclusion, it's different from the misery that comes with the abolition of freedom. It's a very different thing, my friend, this new life I've chosen—how can I explain? I've found it, rediscovered it, traced it out from among all the paths as the only one that counts for me.

Friend, this new life is a flight.

Never, never, not even for a single moment, have I thought, But what have I done? How will time pass? It doesn't pass. The point is that time's an ocean, an entire universe. I pass slowly like someone exploring space and every once in a while I level barriers. What does it matter now if I call myself Alix or Agnes. When I became a novice, after my mother disinherited me, I wanted to change my name. Because in the Saint-Eustache church there was a small chapel, a very old one, they said, in honor of Sainte Agnes, a remote martyr, I chose her name.

At the beginning of my novitiate, I liked to recall my past as a young girl from the Saint-Eustache parish, a woman wearing a mantle, a possessed woman. They said she was someone who had lost everything, who had become free, wandering in the wake of the people and very attached to the city. She was already Agnes when she went up and down the streets, came across bands of wailing children and starved, shabby people waiting for something unidentifiable, when she surprised an old man crouched among mounds of garbage furtively licking some filthy peelings or a cold bone, looking around out of fear of being attacked by hungry dogs. She had become someone who belonged to that part of the river, to that part of the city.

Alix had remained a little out of focus. She was a forgotten Heloise awaiting a birth that never came to be. Over there, beyond the river, she was seated on a low, stone wall looking at the Saint Victor abbey. Alice had remained on the other side. That's all.

Every once in a while I still picture her with a rare book on her knees. She likes the sound of the lute very much; she likes to know that she knows more than her boring and pedantic tutor and that the ancient philosophers are some of the great teachers, tangible footholds to keep disquiet at bay.

Everything else changed quickly; a new horizon hove. Alix became a phantasm. But then, what's important about that? Agnes, too, took her leave.

A strange dance they had; two consciousnesses with their gardens and their markets, a toll paid between one soul and the other, between the city's two eyes. But here, in this center, their run has ended. Once in a while a silent visit is possible, as if one wore different gloves in order to fool the hands. I go along with these doublings of myself in a trinitarian fantasy, retracing my life by bits, in memories. As to the rest, I'm neither one nor the other. I entered into a realm with only one question: Who am I? I am.

Here, I am. My body has become buoyant. Time may hold it as a bud.

It's easy to glide away: a thousand miles between the head and the feet, an ocean between my hands. Another dimension, that's what. It's easy to imagine you're a column or a vertical stairway—first a violet space, then pink, then a yellow one— and easy to feel the boundless deceit of this cell. A construction for repressing what? Tell me, which worlds did they think this wall would keep out?

Every once in a while I hear a distant, very remote music, from where I don't know; at times it becomes an intense sound. A hiss, an excited, incessant whispering. Believe me, the air is full of strange particles that fall in space like drops of rain around us.

I'm not afraid. I'm always thinking of the Thing, the luminous soul. I think, and explore the rest slowly, as if I were an orbiting star.

Look, the cell isn't mine. It's the people outside who are walled in, imprisoned in a flat, animal, clay-like membrane that cuts them off from life.

For me, life began when I bumped against this gristly barrier. When space becomes a network of roads, you can reach out with the hands, swim or fly in every direction. And if you knew how to abolish the barriers, if you were able to see in all directions simultaneously in a single glance, in a turn, a pirouette, an equidistant dance—well then, you'd have begun exploring the city that's beyond all walls. The mundane city reveals itself as a grotesque mockery of the heavenly city. And you ask yourself, But how? How is it possible?

Before the limbs thicken, before the body falls asleep again, that's when you have to decide what to do. If the ideal city is the aspiration of those who demand justice, if the expansion of their consciousness is the goal, if this is the city described by heretics, reformers, preachers, rebels and everybody who is looking to the beyond, to the distant perfect model—well then, it's time to try to make this city possible.

How? I don't know. I'm neither a captain nor an armed rebel. I don't have power over events. I haven't trafficked in matter. I haven't rejected reality, but swallowed it in a way. I want to make my body a bridge, an overarching path.

When I walked on the city's streets—Alix and Agnes were already fused—I thought and reflected on everything I saw. In the face of so much ferocity, I didn't flee. I observed the snares from afar, while sweeping at the Hotel-Dieux, without ever talking. I thought of how everything would have to be different, of how I would want the city to be. And when I went on duty in the refectory, I knew that a bowl of soup and a vague promise was of no use if everything started over in the same way, because the source of misery always regenerated the same misery and the same errors. Really, everything had to be changed.

And of course, "How?" you'll ask. Certainly, what you'd like to say is: "It needs daily insurrections and expansion of the soul." As for the man I'd seen executed in the public square—I believe I now understand why I thought he was a knight, some-one holy. It was because he was a combatant, although he had neither arms nor insignia, neither helmet nor standard. Almost naked, with his hands tied behind his back, alone and standing straight, he had made each muscle and each small bone of his body, each patch of his skin, a weapon. That man was in revolt. His eyes were two catapults aimed at the future. His flesh went to the slaughter vibrating like a platoon of bodies on attack. He was able to launch an alert and fling a challenge with a single muscular contraction.

I'm sure he must have created in those present an endless nightmare, troubled dreams that will be inherited by their de-scendants and the descendants of their descendants, and so on and on, until all doubts are shredded—until the meaning of his revolt is clear to everybody.

Here's change, a mutation. At that moment he made his fight. A man without an army, stripped of his name, not even a hero who will be remembered or vindicated, he fought in his own way, as he could; he fought for all of us for the rest of time.

Yes, yes, sing again, friend, ride across this unmentionable pale. Our roads cross each other's, like the winding circuits of thought.

7

AND WHO ARE YOU?

La danse macabre t'appelle, que chacun 'a danser apprend.
The Dance of Death summons you, instructs each of you to
dance.

> *The initial strophe of the representation of*
> *the "Danse Macabre" painted beneath the*
> *arcades of the Cemetery of the Holy Innocents*
> *one year after the great spectacle that*
> *took place in 1424 in Paris*

TA TATA TATA TA TA, two tambourines, three bagpipes, and
some drums play a measured, cadenced march. The rhythm is
obsessive, always the same.

The spectacle begins at sunrise when the actors and three wagons, led by notables and followed by the curious, gather in front
of the cemetery church portal. After mass, they take to the city
streets, pass over the bridge, and stop in front of the massive
Notre Dame cathedral. There the actors sing some verses and go
through some of the dance steps—just enough to publicize the
spectacle. Then they go back to the streets, heading toward the
university quarter, over the Pont Saint-Michel. Many students
come out, some parodying the actors and their verses; others
dance around the wagons. Slowly, a large crowd assembles.

During the parade, the actors stay on the large bed of the
main wagon. Dressed as the Fool, the Moor skips and recites,
accompanied by a viola that he holds upright with one hand

while flourishing the bow in the air with the other, then nimbly replacing it on the three strings. The other two wagons roll forward silently, one in front and the other behind.

In the lead wagon, the huge head of a whale, black as pitch, slowly opens and closes its mouth as it emerges from the sea. It is made of black papier mâché, and has enormous red lips and pointed teeth made of wood. On a placard placed high on a pole is written HELL'S GULLET, and every once in a while a devil climbs the short hidden stairs, pokes his head out of the whale's mouth, and shakes the bells hanging from his long, shaggy ears.

The last wagon has three rooms set back a little from the wagon bed's edge. The rooms are made with rugs hanging from screens. The three Marys are in one room, crouched and silent, draped in blue mantles. An actor dressed as an angel and holding a lute in his hand, stands next to them. He plays only when the wagons stop and the women stand up.

In the second room, about six feet to a side, there's an actor dressed in a brocade cape that reveals a warrior's armor. He holds a long, thin trumpet in his hand. The people gather around to look at him and declare, "It's the Archangel Michael." "No! It's Gabriel." "Yes, yes, it's he."

In the last room, raised a little higher, is a lone statue of the Virgin, adorned, crowned, and covered with an opaque violet veil. On a placard high above the wagon is written GENTLE REALM. Each time the cortege stops, people applaud and the actors recite verses, repeating them so they won't reveal the plot. Where families or convents have hung carpets and embroidery out of their windows, the procession slows and someone from the balcony declaims an ode to the Virgin or some verses in honor of the actors.

By this time, the wagons have crossed the city and turn back on the way to the cemetery, where guards check to see who has paid, who has passes, and who has hidden weapons. Pregnant women and children are turned away.

While the wagons parade thus through the city's streets, the English regent and court worthies, escorted by dignitaries and soldiers, arrive to the sound of trumpets and bagpipes. The court takes its place on the scaffolding set up along the facade of the church. Festive bells are set ringing and the regent takes his place, accompanied by Princess Isabella in a decorated box. Behind them, the church; in front, the cemetery's large open space. Two jugglers and a ballerina bought as a slave in the Holy Land have come to entertain them, but when the wagons arrive and the public mass under the arcades, the trumpets begin to play and the little company takes its leave.

The wagons slowly enter the cemetery from the wide, side entrance, passing in front of the court's dais, crossing the entire cemetery diagonally in order to draw up in front of the central arch of the Charnier des Esclaves. The largest wagon takes the center, the other two to each side of it.

The actors are hidden behind and under the wagons. The public is gathered around, held back by beams that create a small clearing. Some workers run quickly under the stage and the musicians get ready. The people watch attentively.

Then the music begins. The unseen orchestra plays behind a tent hidden by the main wagon.

Ta tata tata ta ta: a sustained rhythm like one that precedes a battle.

From the central wagon draped in black something emerges from the bed with slow, regular thrusts. It's a mass of coarse hair. A head. Slowly the rest of the body shows itself. A skinny, nude body draped in white linen, and from the shroud hangs a bloodied pelt. The people murmur, shout, applaud. The trick of the mechanical stool has worked. Death leaps up, spreads his arms, stretches his legs, and sticks out his tongue as he bends down. He dances smartly with cadenced leaps and then suddenly stops, shaking only his shoulders in a convulsive tremor. He stops dead still, flat on his feet, his arms held close to the length of his body; he turns, turns back. Keeping a stiff neck, he moves his head, first right, then left. The music's tempo increases incessantly. Many times he repeats the movement in rhythm with his shoulders, then once again he leaps in the other direction, his legs half-bent in order to return to an unmoving, upright stance, shaking his shoulders to the obsessive rhythm of the fifes and drums. The music keeps its beat— threatening, hypnotizing. Then suddenly, silence. Very slowly he goes back down the hidden hole in the wagon bed.

Now the Moor arrives. In total silence, he climbs to the stage by stairs at the side of the wagon. He bows. In his hand he hold the same three-stringed instrument he had played in the morning. He is dressed in a dark coverall and carries a cap with bells. On a placard behind him is printed, DEATHS FOOL. The three Marys come from their cart dressed in long blue capes. Their shoulder-length hair hangs loosely. Barefooted, they take a step forward holding hands. They say, "And who are you?"

The Fool answers, playing his instrument and intimating some dance steps:

I am the clown, I am the crazy,
I am the blockhead and the obsessed.
I am the conscience of the dead
not the skull, but the living heart of man.
I am the comrade of the missing
the juggler for the great buffoon.
I act out the question, dance the answer
at the threshold of every door.
I summon you and follow the crowd
of the living—and the dead.

He has just finished reciting these lines when the audience hears cries in the distance, and a galloping sound. From the far side of the arcades a horse comes racing; nude Death is in the saddle, ranting, whipping the horse to make it run still faster. The audience is surprised, amazed, and pleased. The dignitaries applaud, and all the actors scurry from under the wagons, rush into the clearing, and begin dancing wildly to form a circle around the horse. Death dismounts; someone covers him with a shroud, and he returns to the wagon-bed stage while the Fool takes his place as narrator at the side. When he raises his hands, the people quiet down and pay attention. The actors have all disappeared again under and behind the wagons. Silence. The three Marys come forward.

Everything is held in readiness for the major actor. The Fool signals from afar, repeatedly calls him and says:

Here he is, he comes to us, in gold and crimson.
Here is the Pope, the chosen one,
unmatched by any, the peerless one.

From the far side of the central stage, a manikin enters. Manipulated from behind with a pole, it is sumptuously dressed in crimson velvet with gilded lace. The manikin shuffles along, takes a few stiff bows and heads toward Death. It is followed by a figure in a black coverall, who is the actor playing the part of the Pope's skeleton. The actor takes mincing steps, skipping and jerking to mime the slow course of the manikin.

From the distance, one of the three Marys wails:

Which is the living one, which is the dead?

The actor answers, half-hidden behind the manikin's cape:

I am he who is, he who was.
Gone the papal tiara, gone the prelate's surplice.
I am only a body without flesh—
what he had forgotten he would be.

The Fool comes forward with raised hands, bows to the audience:

The Pope alive, the Pope dead.
Watch and heed this simpleton.
The Lord will judge, the Lord will tell us
to which kingdom he will have to go.

Smoke comes out of the whale's mouth and devils run and dance along while the sound of a lute comes from the wagon. Death strides up and shouts:

Ah, no! No, indeed! My dead one I won't let go!
With me nine days he'll have to stay.

With a skip Death seizes the Pope manikin and hangs him from a hook on the stage while the actor playing the Pope's skeleton takes a leap and stands motionless beside the pendant Pope. Death is now going off shaking and tugging at his coarse hair. He leans forward as if to look at someone far away.

With a roll of drums, a second manikin enters followed by his double. The Fool introduces him:

Ah! here is the great King, who commands everything.
He has no more knaves, and a court no more.
Who will restrain Death if it's mightier than he?

One of the three Marys sings from her wagon:

Where is the body to bury, the body for burial.
Where is the shroud, the winding sheet to wrap?

The King's double enters; he is dressed like the other skeleton in a black coverall marked by some white dashes for bones. He halts, waits for the crowned manikin that is slowly moving along. He hides behind it and follows it to the sound of the bagpipes until he reaches the figure of Death. The Fool raises his hands, asks for silence and turns to the audience to introduce the new character.

The Lombard can't concentrate. He's agitated, restless. He looks at the scene but the spectacle bores him despite the Fool's splendid performance.

He is pleased only when the three young actresses move forward with tiny steps and sing, rocking back and forth. So the Lombard decides to leave, and as he makes his way through the crowd, he suddenly has the strange sensation that someone is looking at him from behind, spying on him. He turns his head and sees a figure half-hidden in the crowd. Is it the Gascon he glimpses? He hurries away as the voices from the spectacle grow more confused and he hears only indistinct sentences.

It's the Knight's turn to enter; and the actor playing him complains:

Ah, my body torn from this earth and captured,
taken from my Lady, from my Lady sundered.

The three Marys say:

Where is the body, where is the body to wash?

Passing by the fountain, the Lombard feels a tug on his hand. It's the Turnip, leaning on his beggar friend the Baby and standing on a marble ledge in order to see better and, at the same time, to ask for alms without being trampled.

"Lombard! Finally you've come by. It's hard to find you in this crowd. I've been looking for you. And so has the Gascon. Listen, you must leave, and don't waste time. Don't wait for the pilgrims. Leave here immediately. The Gascon's organized. He's the absolute boss here, like I told you. He controls all the beggars, has his informers spy on them. Baby and I are your friends, in memory of the Big Turk. I haven't forgotten the night you saved me when they were about to smash me in the dirt like a worm. But we can't stay long. They watch us, and it will be difficult to get near you again. I'm afraid. Everything I earn is counted and doesn't belong to me. I'm only given enough to keep me from dying of hunger and for the permit that lets me stay here. What else can I do? Saint Quentin of the Crippled! Get out of here before the play ends. Escape!"

Changing expression, the Turnip returns to begging, reciting his litanies, and hanging tight to Baby's back.

Leave? thinks the Lombard. For where? The pilgrims don't assemble until tomorrow. I came on Ash Wednesday. It seems impossible that I've been here only one week. It seems like I've been here for so long, and I've come so far, fooling myself into believing it might be important. A pilgrimage. But why, if it's against my people's teachings? And now there's the Gascon looking for me, but what can he have against me? The Big Turk told me to be careful, that one is tricky, a coward, a brigand. And what if, out of malevolence, he were the double of the Fool? What if he had the idea of a spectacle to make me lose my mind so I couldn't find the way out? Is he a sorcerer? Or a phantasm? What's his game? What's real? Is this a farce? A confused nightmare? Damn, the Bohemian will think I'm crazy. He has such a clear conscious plan. He who came a long way from a victorious country in rebellion can master the ambushes in this cursed place. My plan used to be clear, too, the plan of a young man on the road. But something has broken loose now.

I sense chaos, that's what it is. Going in and out of the tents, I thought, Where's the inside? And where's the outside? Am I coming out or going into a room? Am I someone who came by accident, or was I anticipated, and prepared? That's the impression I have now, the feeling of being foreseen in a grand celebration. Everything I've done, said, everything I've thought was a carefully readied poem. Good God! Maybe I'm the one who must die. The Gascon deceives, sends me messages and warnings, says he wants to kill me, but really only wants to see how I'll react. He knows if I will die or not."

The Lombard looks around, then leans back against the column, mentally addressing the woman in the wall: Why didn't you answer me this morning. I went down to your cell at sunrise. I called out to you. I told you the story of my life. Then I asked you for a sign, one very small sign, which might tell me what I must do. But you didn't answer. I stayed there a long time, until the wagons left and with them all the curiosity seekers. I waited in that quiet space until noon. But you didn't show a sign of life. Yet I thought if only I could say to you, "The lover is kept a prisoner outside your walls. I am he." I would have said, "I am the lover separated from his beloved. Here he is. Here is the perfect lover who has reached you after having passed through every danger, every trial—alien lands, circles of hell, abysses. He doesn't ask you to show yourself, he doesn't want to touch you. No, he wants only a sign, a token that seals our encounter." But you didn't answer.

The drum rolls startle the Lombard, who, immersed in his thoughts, is fixed on the distant cell. Maybe it's because of this spectacle that I'm so edgy today, he thinks. The Moor is a great actor. If I were to jump on the stage, how would I present myself? Who would I be? Would the Marys say, "Where is the body, where is the body that . . . ?"

Suddenly, the excited crowd cries out and the Lombard looks toward the stage, where a young woman enters the scene. What? A woman! The Lombard shifts around to get a better look. He is alert, completely absorbed in the distant figure of the young actress, who comes forward.

The lady is dressed in a scarlet corset, tight on her delicate body, and a bonnet covers her hair, forehead and neck, exposing an oval, pale face. She uses yellow gold voile for a scarf. A violet cape lightly trails from her shoulders. A wooden manikin in the form of a skeleton manipulated from behind follows her, wobbling and crackling like the sound of dry bones.

The Lombard is caught up and joins the audience in order to hear better. He thinks he catches a whiff of the wet, grassy wind of some days earlier, a wind suspended in mid-air, carrying with it imperceptible odors, a summer wind that eddies unnoticed among the sickly-sweet, heavy odors of the cemetery. Death, bent forward, legs spread apart, waits for the young woman at center stage. His coarse hair is in wild disarray. In a cavernous voice he says:

Come, my pretty damsel, come dance the tarantella!

One of the three Marys from another wagon sings, slowly swaying:

Where is the body that discloses the beautiful soul to be saved?

Death approaches the young woman, dancing obscenely around her, sticking out his tongue and belching. Then he grasps her arm and sings in a low voice:

I am the one whom all avoid, always ready for those who falter.
Tell me, where is your lover who will free you from my clutch?

The young woman interrupts him. She sings, but without looking at him, standing steady and composed at center stage. Death pulls back, surprised. She sings:

My perfumed body belongs to a lover in a radiant sphere alien to you.

The Fool springs forward, leaping and pirouetting, and with a half-serious sneer cries, as Death might taunt:

Quiet, quiet hapless one, whom Death has impaled.
To the gallant he denies abduction of his lover.
To the maiden he denies defiance of his command.
Great Death has no equal in a world of witless ones,
for he alone is armed.

But the young woman is absorbed in her song and is unshaken; she spreads her arms wide and sings:

This maiden's in a brighter land
for Love defies dark Death's command.

Death screams, pulls his hair, seizes her from behind in a mighty grip and drags her toward the manikins.

Strange, very strange, thinks the Lombard, walking away.

"Friend," a voice breaks in. The Bohemian is standing next to him. "Do you like the play? I looked for you among all these people. Every time I thought I'd found you, it turned out it wasn't you. And look at how many came, at how much enthusiasm there is. But then if you take someone aside and say to him, 'You're a corpse,' he's mightily offended and he hits you. Doesn't this seem strange to you?"

The Lombard nods his assent. The Bohemian is always right, he thinks. He always notices the most important thing. He is always to the point and knows what to emphasize and how to anticipate reality. If he were to know how I reason, like a distant echo that reverberates with sounds and images but can no longer distinguish reality from the echo of the echo, if he knew that, he couldn't understand it. Or maybe he does know. In fact, there's no doubt he knows.

"I don't like this Mystery," continues the Bohemian. "It seems a giant swindle. After all, the ugly one isn't death, and these people are alive and well—these dignitaries, everybody here. Let's even say that the shivers are well made, that the actors are first rate and please the people because they say, "You're a corpse!" to the most powerful of the powerful. But wouldn't it be better if the equality in death were granted in life? I would say, in fact, to every living thing. I think the crowd is watching the parody of hope. Dark hope. What about the real truth? How do you judge what the king and all the powerful ones here do?"

The Lombard nods yes again. Damn the Bohemian. With one stroke he lays everybody out, strips them naked, while I nearly always let myself be moved by my feelings.

"And the Lady who defies Death?" the Lombard dares to ask.

"Which Lady?" answers the Bohemian fixing his gaze on the Lombard through half-closed eyes.

Then, without waiting for an answer, he resumes talking in a low voice and leans toward the Lombard. "Despite the cold and dampness of this spring's Lent, I feel hot and oppressed. Let's say that this place has its effect on me, too. Friend, who has bewitched us? Or is this feeling of confusion normal, because it's the most accursed place I've ever seen. Let's go get a drink of water, far away from all these actors of rack and ruin. The play will last until evening. They have to cover the thirty professions of man and will end, they told me, with a grand cavalcade. The people will be so impressed that, after the excitement of an afternoon, they will be able to go back to their horrible lives. Let's say they will have had the thrill of an ancient, malignant parable."

The Lombard follows him. They make their way through the spectators, moving away from the people massed around the wooden stage. To avoid an old fat woman who wipes her face with a rag, the Lombard is aware that he has grabbed the Gascon's arm. Damn, he thinks. But the Gascon's dry, wrinkled face is averted. He is alert, attentive, yet seems not to have noticed the Lombard.

Is he here by chance or has he been waiting for me, wonders the Lombard. Maybe he's got the skewer hidden in his hand. Could that be?

But the Gascon doesn't move, doesn't look around. The Lombard crosses the path of a toothless man who yawns and, elbowing his companion, says, "They might have given us a lass on this patrol, a buxom dancer . . . ."

The Lombard wipes his forehead; he's shaking. Hallucinations. The echo of the echo. Misinterpreting. I feel tired, so tired.

Already seated some distance away, against the wall under the arcade, the Bohemian drinks from a small cup of water. The Lombard sits down next him without saying anything. He holds the little bowlful of water the Bohemian has handed him, but he has no desire to drink.

"What's got hold of you, friend? What makes you so serious? You're not the least impressed by this farce!"

"No, no, that's not it. It's a certain confusion. I don't know if I'll be able to tell you the truth. In comparison to you, I'm a naive boy who believed he knew a lot. Yet, I spend all my time trying to give meaning to the world's events. I'm a young heretic on a quest. But I've lost confidence. At the same time, a strange thing is happening to me. Inside me and surrounding me I feel some things that give me an ineffable feeling of strength, of energy."

The Bohemian calmly answers, "Oh, it's all a question of perspective. You're still missing some steps."

The lines on his cheeks crowd around his eyes, balancing with respect to his face's axis, and the Lombard thinks: This time the smile has perfectly expressed his thought, as if he had wanted to give concrete proof of a geometry problem! The Lombard feels more tranquil. That man, so crystal clear and sure of his judgments, makes him feel less uneasy. The Bohemian has a rare warmth.

"Listen to me, Lombard. What do you go seeking in the world if your land needs remaking, if your people's land has been occupied three times?"

"Three times?" repeats the Lombard.

"Look at this cemetery. There are the dead, the stage players, the foreign soldiers as well the people of this city. It's a defeated land."

The Lombard nods assent.

"Yet," continues the Bohemian, "sometimes a little thing is enough, like that ragged sack of salt, to change everything. In my country, who would have expected that someone, the man for a new world, would come from the village of Husinec to alert the people and create an explosion? To free yourself is not an easy thing, but in the long run, you know the right ideas are contagious. Like the plague, but in another sense. These stupid bastards believe the plague is carried by lepers, Jews, Spanish gypsies, and heretics. The cowards drive them out, throw them down wells, tear them into little pieces. What does their cruelty change? Until we realize that there's an understanding between heaven and man that works through our consciousness, and that consciousness, our conscience, metes out good and evil in our material, concrete actions, nothing in this lower world will change. A sympathizing heretic? All right, and I'll add, I am a Husite notary faithful to a universal, spiritual religion."

The Bohemian whispers these last words under his breath, leaning close to the Lombard. He closes his eyes. Seen thus, in profile, with his long, nearly white hair, the pouches puffy under his eyes, the Bohemian seems old. Perhaps he's tired, too, thinks the Lombard. But the conscripted pilgrim under ban has no choice, and it's best for him not to entertain any doubts. He has but one destination and a single aim.

The Bohemian opens his eyes. "But where do you want to go? On a pilgrimage? And why ever do that? Looking for the truth in a place, a relic, or a saint, can be illusory. Your great-grandparents said it clearly: Don't go on pilgrimages, don't create idols, don't worship any kind of material thing."

"Yes, they told me not to tip my cap to anyone. For them the Church was the devil's tool, the mass a snare, and the bishop a greedy man guilty of carnal vices. My grandparents were poor by choice. They didn't eat meat, they didn't swear or kill, nor did they respect reliquaries or saints. They read the gospels to each other and entrusted themselves to the authority of the Just. As a child I heard them talking about all these things and I heard accounts of strange facts. I remember underground secrets, stories of initiations and persecutions. After that, growing up in Novara, where my people emigrated, I noticed that things had changed. People were afraid of the Inquisition and were in the habit of pretending. Later, I wanted to study. I was ambitious and wanted to forget that whole Waldensian family spread out in the mountains, knocked from here to there, persecuted, burned at the stake by the Inquisitors. So as you know, being an orphan, I left."

"Fine. Going away is always good, walking, just walking. But your soul is the more important factor. Why do you think the Inquisitors have been ruthless to your people? Because those peasants and artisans refuse to bow down, refuse to let themselves be run by greedy strangers who are always ready to sell relics and indulgences of every kind, because they want to keep to themselves with God without seals of approval. Perhaps you too should be firmer in will. You expect to find the truth on the way to Compostella, but the answer is always within you!"

The Bohemian closes his eyes again, and slowly drinks some water. He says, then, "Thus you would have a vision of the soul that only you can see, because it would come from within yourself."

With the little cup in hand, the Bohemian takes a few sips as the water seller disappears again in the crowd. His helper, a small, scurrying boy, comes up to the Bohemian, takes the money, and carries away the cup after the Lombard has also drunk.

Then, the old woman followed by her silent daughter, who had accosted the Lombard the day before, approaches them and says, "Well, you have a different friend and you don't introduce him to me." She casts a searching look at the Bohemian, but the Lombard has the impression that the old woman is insincere and speaking ironically.

"So he's a pilgrim, too? And he's also taken a vow of chastity? Mother of mine, nothing's happening here with you two. But I'm not worried. Today, while that Fool goes about his business making sheep's eyes, I'm raising and lowering my skirt behind the columns and the bushes. Look, like this! Ashamed? It's the money, my handsome one, it's the money that's important to me. I don't want to end up in the common grave. With the permission of the canon, I'm having a tomb made in this ground that cradled me. When they were sticking my mother in the ground—they threw her away like a bitch—they heard my wail. The truth is my mother was still giving birth to me even if she was dead. Or maybe she wasn't. I don't know. The only thing I know is that the sacristan's wife brought me up. I was born more from the earth than from my mother. And you expect me to die without a beautiful sculpture? I'm having it made for me, even if I don't have as much money as the Gascon.

"I keep company with my daughter, but he hangs around with miserable, luckless wretches, commanding everybody and pulling their strings as if they were manikins. He has a court, his secretary, his valets, and his couriers. But it's all secret. They talk in gestures no one can understand. It's really a secret society, for he gives orders from a distance with a sign and a wink. Anyone who betrays him is assassinated, and he always does it with his own hand. It's his Rule. Everything always goes smoothly; no one here notices anything. No one has time to bother with it.

"On this holy ground the laws are turned upside down, even more than outside the walls. You'll come to understand better than you do now! Here, everyone has the right of asylum; everyone mingles, but the problem is to stay here for long, because if you decide to stay, you have to obey the Rule. Now, he's the one who commands; hence, the Rule is his.

"You're the first stranger who's stuck his nose in the Gascon's business and you may have thought for good reasons. But who's doing anything to you, my handsome one? There's something in you I wouldn't trust. You interfered in a row. You knew who killed the Saracen. You made a friend of his worst enemy, and you're seen with this one and that one. You were there when he killed the Big Turk. None of this can be to the Gascon's liking. But, he doesn't give me orders. Like Joshua, I was here from the start, and I have my Rule too.

"It's not long since the Gascon came, but the moment he got here he started waiting. He watched Joshua and waited, waited for his treasure to grow. He hoped to take it and escape with it, because they said Joshua had some alchemists' protective dust. And how did that end up? Joshua's dead—incredible, but true. Dead of natural causes. No one knows where he kept his treasure; and if he gave it to somebody, no one knows who has it. The Saracen was his friend and he's dead, and the Big Turk, too. The Gascon's like a fox now, sniffing and sniffing, going crazy trying to find the treasure. Is there one or not? Does one of Joshua's friends know about it? You know. You made a friend of the Big Turk.

"But I go on. You all make me laugh. What's it to me? I'm the mistress of this ground, not the woman in the wall. She knows nothing. Nothing about treasure! I saw you this morning by her cell. What did you think you'd discover? If she knows anything, she'll tell it to the confessor, the confessor to the sacristan, and the sacristan to the Gascon. What were you thinking?"

Every time the old woman mentions the woman sealed in the wall, the Lombard feels nauseated. No, he thinks, the walled-in woman is well protected; she's in her cell.

If the Lombard is so interested in the recluse it's not only because she's a mysterious figure whose life story and visions he would have liked to know in every detail as a Platonic symbol or the perfect allegory, but also because he feels strangely close to her. She, too, suffers from the pathos of an epoch.

So, the woman in the wall is making her own fight in this way, thinks the Lombard, by carrying on a long, invisible expedition with victories and defeats in this thrice-conquered land—or in another world. We know about the visible battles; the chronicles bequeathed us are part of history, but maybe she's started something that will leave traces only in . . .

Interrupted by the roll of drums, the Lombard is distracted and looks at the stage, then falls into thought again, pleased to have possibly found the answer to a puzzle, one of those metaphysical responses to the struggle between good and evil that would have pleased the Just Ones. Then he shakes his head: But why must I try to explain my decision?

There is, in fact, *no* explanation if it's not that of an historical contest between a reality and an individual, in this case a young woman just as tenacious and vulnerable as the Lombard. In this age of contradictions, even an unusual man like the Bohemian—a Husite communist, who comes from a people in revolt, and a spokesman for the lay pietism of the Brothers of Christ's Law—is also one who's looking for absolute answers. Otherwise, he thinks, we'd be matter without a mind.

So different in education and origins, yet all seekers and visionaries—Alix/Agnes, the Lombard, and the Bohemian. They were absorbed in strange monologues, and it's not by mere chance that they harbored the same ideas and the same hopes, because the need for something new was overwhelming. Their world needed to move on, to change.

The old hag makes a gesture and says, "I'm going now. Don't waste my time. There's a lot about you I don't like. You listen but pay no mind."

"Not so," exclaims the Lombard, pulling on her arm. "There's something you must tell me. What game is the Turnip playing in this story?"

"The Turnip? That hobbling leftover! There's something in him I wouldn't trust. Panicked people always let the cat out of the bag. What's he telling you? That the Gascon's looking for you? Maybe he's the one who's looking for you. Everybody's hunting. The Turnip is telling you this that so you'll tell him where the treasure is, and then he'll take off on Baby's rump. He tells you to leave and then he sets a trap for you. Ah! How many queer things we see nowadays."

The crone looks sideways at him, baring her rotting teeth, "If you want to tell me, my little one, you can be sure you'll be safe under my Rule and we'll make a splendid family. What more could you want?"

The Lombard suddenly stands up. He has to close his eyes because he feels dizzy. To stay here, he thinks, working for the Gascon and training the Turnip, pimping for the daughter, dispatching the Baby to horny old men? Shaving fat from cadavers at night and looking for treasure in the graves? He feels a chill. Is there no alternative to the Rule here or elsewhere? Inside here. Outside there. Pilgrim, vagabond, orphan, outsider—none of this can protect me from this cursed game.

He looks the old woman in eyes and shouts, "Listen, I have no treasure. No one has spoken to me about treasure and I don't care about it. The Big Turk had better things on his mind. You're all miserable! You're all wrong about everything. Treasure! For me the soul is a treasure. That's right. But what does that mean to you? You can't touch it or smell it. It doesn't clink or shine like money. The soul is remote and invisible. Good God! Leave me in peace!"

The Lombard is trembling. He sits back down, talking wildly. "Everybody wants something from me, but I don't know what. Or else they want me to go crazy because I don't belong to any Rule. And now I find myself involved in some kind of game."

The Bohemian rests his head against the wall and doesn't move; his serious face imperturbable. He seems to be asleep. The old hag shouts as she leaves, "You'll see. You'll see how you'll need me."

"We hope not!" the Bohemian exclaims suddenly, opening his eyes. "Let's just say that the time for you to leave has come, understand? We have to get out of here and in a hurry. The quicker the better. I don't like that old witch."

But the Lombard doesn't move. He doesn't understand the Bohemian's swift reaction.

"Of course you have to go," insists the Bohemian, "because if the witch is wrong, it means the Gascon is really out to kill you.

And if she's right, it means the Turnip lied to you and thinks you really do have a treasure. And if he believes it, so does the Gascon. It's a vicious circle. The beginning and the end are the same in the chaotic minds of these people. They're all gripped by deceit and can't escape.

"Your tenacity has forced the vicious circle into the open. You can feel satisfied. Now do you understand what I told you last night? I said that your friend the Big Turk had found a treasure where there was nothing but salt. But the Gascon—since he's looking for that sack he thinks is full of gold coins—will find only some salt in the very place where there's an invisible treasure! This is the story that made me laugh yesterday and that appealed to me very much, yes, very much indeed."

"How do you know all this?" asks the Lombard.

But the Bohemian doesn't answer. He stands up and replies, "Wait here for me. I'm going to get our things from the caretaker, and when I get back, we'll leave before the spectacle ends."

The insistent, obsessive music starts up again. The last manikin passes in front of Death. The spectacle is nearing the end. All the dead in black costumes are dancing a wild rondo while the manikins suspended at the back of the stage are jittering, shaken by so much frenetic action. The audience murmurs, "Here it comes, here it comes. The rondo, the great dance, begins." Those who had fallen asleep abruptly woke up and carefully adjusted their berets. Those who drifted off to sit along the wall, and men who had entertained themselves with a woman, came back to the railings.

"Get up! Wake up! The best part's coming," shouts a small, half-blind fat man wending his way happily through the audience. His spreading cries reanimate the crowd. All the devils come out of the whale's mouth, and smoke comes out of two holes that are the papier mâché monster's ugly nostrils. The horned devils shake their little bells and stick out their tongues.

Then when the dance of the dead and the devils comes to a halt, the three Marys step forward to the sound of Gabriel's trumpet. The young women spread their arms, slowly shaking their hair, throw their cobalt blue capes behind them, join hands and sing. The Lombard can't hear their words distinctly, but he watches Gabriel who comes into the Virgin's room and very slowly lifts the veil that covers her.

It's a statue dressed in ample, sumptuous silk. It seems like a precious pyramid from which only the hands and face are showing. She has a fleshy, petrified face, painted with vivid colors, and her large black eyes bulge out in a fixed gaze. People whisper, "How beautiful! Holy Virgin, our Lady, Divine Mother." With deep emotion, they make the sign of the cross. Some think it resembles the Black Virgin of Saint-Germain who is the Sainte-Sara-des-Gitans. A man blurts out, "Here is the jolly Saint Hautain," and claps his thigh in appreciation. People silence him.

The Seraphim and the angels from the GENTLE KINGDOM play the lute. Then a great quiet, a feeling of sadness, imbues the scene. Everyone, deeply affected, contemplates the lighted statue of the Virgin covered with jewels and silvered veils, around which the Seraphim is lighting candles. The people continue to make comments, carefully examining her face. When Gabriel, standing tall in his armor, sounds his trumpet again, the veil falls and covers the statue once more.

The three Marys move off, still singing:

And who are you, dear friend, our brother, unknown man?
Our sister, lost woman, who are you, our unknown friend?"

The Fool, raising his hands and disappearing little by little on the hidden stool that lowers beneath the wagon, concludes:

If to this question, there's no reply,
the beautiful soul abides in hiding.

Each actor descends from the stage in the square, holding his own decorated manikin by the hand, and starts to dance. Death, nude except for strips of bloody hide, returns on horseback from afar. The actors throw their doubles at his feet, making a heap of objects—crowns, outstretched arms, torn cords—that the horse tramples while everyone dances.

The effect is powerful. The crowd cheers, people make the sign of the cross and kneel along the course run by the galloping horse.

Oh, yes, thinks the Lombard, who has observed the final scene from a distance, a fitting statue—as if a piece of plastered wood could be the image of divine love. If a material object can embody it, why not? It's better that these people use wood to make images instead of gallows. My God, love for the beloved is something else. It's what those devotees of love, the Fidèle d'Amour, demand, as do those of us who yearn for a sign that will kindle us. But these people only understand appearances.

Lost in his thoughts, the Lombard no longer pays attention to the spectacle. Here I am in the belly of the human family, beset by doubts and snares. Why has my voyage brought me to this road that takes me back to the world? The Bohemian would say to a land thrice conquered. Yes, and where has he gone now? Why is he taking so long?"

Had something happened to his friend in the confusion of the spectators' frenetic dance. The Lombard is feeling anxious; he's made the decision to leave: I'm certain the Gascon's looking for me, and maybe the Turnip tells me to get away because he's made a deal with someone who's waiting for me at the cemetery gate. And the old crone—when she told me about the treasure, there was a strange glint in her eyes. Does she work for the Gascon, too?

Restless and tense, he keeps walking back and forth along the wall when he hears, "Lombard! Lombard!" He starts, and turns, but sees no one.

"Psst! Here, under the stall." It's the Turnip, crouched behind a scrivener's closed counter.

"But why are you still here? This is exactly where the Gascon will come, not at the entrance where the guards are. I came in a hurry. Not even the Baby came with me. He thinks I'm pissing behind a column and, besides, he's busy trying to hide a few coins from the master. I'm risking my life to warn you. It's very serious. The Gascon sent the old woman to you in person. They work together, he under his Rule, she under hers.

"The Big Turk was right, you are soft-hearted! Lombard, my friend, I'm saying this for laughs, but don't you have legs? By all the saints, then, run away and see the world for me, who can barely crawl. If you die, the Gascon will say he defended the church from a dangerous heretic. Why do you keep going around saying what you believe? Even the stones have ears here."

The Turnip's dark eyes under his protruding brow are the moist, shifting eyes of a man accustomed to fleeing, eyes that retain something infantile. What a life he must have had, thinks the Lombard, a life passed ducking feet, spit, ditches. Mocked, covered with greasy rags. He probably doesn't even remember his last caress. For heaven's sake, maybe he has never been *seen*. If he's lying to me, all right. I won't tell him that I discovered his game. For a moment, the Turnip's eyes narrow, hinting at an understanding, an inner warmth.

"Really, Lombard, why aren't you careful, instead of going around talking about heresies. I saw you with the Bohemian, too, you know."

"The Bohemian!" The Lombard grabs him by the arm, and begins to shake him. He can't control himself. He cries, "Brother, listen, that's enough. If all of you want to drive me crazy, all right, but if you want to make me doubt everybody, you're wrong. Ideas, too, must count for something. Get away from me!"

"Calm yourself, by Saint Quentin. Calm down. I'm a friend. Have you understood that or not? The Bohemian, well, the Bohemian is an old acquaintance."

This is it, thinks the Lombard. As he moves closer to the Turnip to ask him to explain, he hears footsteps. Someone's coming.

"Yes, I am an old acquaintance. The Turnip's right. In fact, let's say that the Turnip doesn't completely lie." The Bohemian is standing there, his long hair almost transparent. Against the light, his figure seems slightly corroded, like an ancient drawing excavated by worms. Suddenly he seems older, more tired. How serious he looks, and sad. Who is he, anyway? The Lombard's hands are cold and damp. For a long moment he is immobile and can't think clearly.

"You look pale, but don't worry. I'm not an agent or a spy. Believe me, what I told you is true and everything of which I spoke happened, except that I came to Paris four years ago and never left for Rome. I stayed. I began to come here regularly at every assembly, in order not to arouse the suspicions of the ecclesiastical tribunal. I'm always saying I'll leave.

"Yes, I knew the Big Turk. A beautiful spirit. Why haven't I left? All right, I'll tell you now that I know you're not a spy. I've never gone because I've never repented. That's why."

The Bohemian sits down and leans against the counter as the Turnip disappears under the beams of the crate.

"I'm old. I'm sixty. Life has tried me and exhausted me. How much time do I have to live? Not much. I've added things up and I said "no" to myself. For me to repent would have been cowardly; to finish a dangerous journey, madness. Return to my people? How could I? I'm a notary without papers, a pilgrim always and forever, banished until I die. Every once in a while I feel a deep longing, something deep in my bones that roils my body with grief. But I can't go back. History is long, each has his road to follow, and every once in a while there's a rest stop.

"When I saw you the other day I recognized you—the new kind of young man, a man of the new generation capable of looking at the events of our time and unmasking them. That's the reason I introduced myself. I wanted to talk with you. I sensed a light in you, a vital force. And it's not by accident that you're a Waldensian who bumped into a Bohemian. Our ideas, friend, are contagious. And then, I noticed that you were in danger. I saw you the night you intervened in the fight against the Gascon. That night I'd come by chance to pretend, like always, to get ready for my departure. Then I saw how shaken you were, friend, and, as I said, had rooted chaos out into the open.

"Now it's you who has to leave. The Turnip knows that. He won't betray you. But give him the Big Turk's sack of salt so the Baby can deliver it to the Gascon. That way you'll be able to leave without fear; you'll have proved your honesty. Because that sack is what he's looking for.

"Here are your things, your bag, your staff. I hope you'll excuse me, but I had to sample this famous salt. Really salt, all right. What a nose the Big Turk had—salt wrapped in a rag for spice traders. You can smell the ginger and the resin.

"Exotic odors, dust from a dry root and dust from a coagulating gum, a coincidence in the life of objects. Let's just say, apparently coincidences, because the gypsy Bohemians who read the cards say there are no coincidences, only correspondences between objects and facts. It would seem that in this unsettled world, in this primordial disorder, not only good and evil, not only people, but also objects have their court and their messengers. That's why you must be able to distinguish one thing from another. Now it's no longer a question of dreaming, Lombard, no longer a matter of defeating appearances. Let's say you have to master life like you tame a dragon. After all, here there are not only messengers from the Gascon and Inquisitors who spy on the people. There are also messengers from the future. Why must they all come from the past?"

The Bohemian stands up and readjusts his black cape. "As you see, I'm not such a logical notary as you think, but I am rational by conviction and heretical by passion. I'm an unrepentant old man who carries with him the magic world of Prague, its dark streets filled with golems, vagabond philosophers, and men in revolt. Friend, I shall never forget our meeting."

With a quiet, natural movement, he puts his hands on the Lombard's head in a barely perceptible gesture. Half closing his eyes to show he understands, he adds, "You're right, the sealed-in woman is . . . ." He murmurs something indistinct and then he disappears in the crowd.

The Lombard feels someone tugging his arm. The Turnip whispers, "I have to go, too. The play is done. Get up, help me out of here. That's right, well done. Yes, I'll give him the sack of salt. I'll arrange things. A great brain that Bohemian. I see you've already got your staff and bag in hand. Let me give you this to remember me by. Take it, but don't ask me where I got it. I promise you I didn't steal it. It belonged to one of the actors from the Dance throng. Keep it, and go. Run for me, let everyone see it."

The Turnip shakes his hand, his two black eyes shining. Then he disappears, hurrying along the arcade toward the bushes, adroitly supporting himself with his hands.

But look at what he's given me! thinks the Lombard. A hat. A splendid hat. Not a pilgrim's hat, not a beret or a cowl, but a felt hat, wide and black. It's a hat like those peasants from Certosa wear, a bandit's hat. No, not a hat for a brigand, but for someone banished, cast out, exiled with horse and sling.

Yes, I'm going. You'll understand me. If I had gone on a pilgrimage to Compostella, I would have stayed the same person, a man plus a hat, an illusion, a false certainty. Rather than dying by the Gascon's skewer, or betrayed by a rogue pilgrim, I'm joining my people beyond the slopes of Certosa. If I have to die, I'll die striving to throw off our triple oppression, die free, fighting for a new world.

8

A L I X ' S   T H I R D   S O L I L O Q U Y

In this vast silence surrounded by the cry for war, hidden outside the fleeting mirage of time, the unremitting victor hates the sound of other silences. But because it has destroyed the illusion of not being alone, the loneliness of being alone is no more.

—René Daumal

SOME THINGS ARE LIKE a spider's web strung between plants. Seen straight on, the web is so transparent that you can't see it; you look through it instead. It's quite different when threads stick to you, when threads you walk through cling to you and surprise you. But glimpsed from an angle when the light strikes it diagonally, you can easily discern the web.

Webs, woven in a vacuum, raise an imperceptible barrier between plants.

From my cell's small opening, looking from a certain angle in the evening, when it's lighted by torch or the moon, the cemetery square seems to me like a vacuum inhabited by strange dramas and strange weavers, a strategy of lines and ties shooting out between the walls and the fountain. There's a grassy area on which people have walked in all directions for centuries, leaving worn paths and yellowed tracks.

Yesterday I was thinking about all this while I watched from

my cell. It was already late and totally dark. I'd thought of a
spider web I'd noticed long ago. That day I was running in a
field and by a happy accident, under the trees where the light
fell diagonally, I saw an immense spider web on a bush in the
sunlight. I stopped. I stayed there looking at that curious thing,
a well-woven trap just waiting for a bee, a moth, or a fly. I found
it curious because I had always thought of a spider web as a
work of damp darkness. To find it thus in the open air in the
vegetable kingdom and in an unexpected place surprised me.
Had nature lured it here or has the web deceived nature, I asked
myself.

The evening before last, when I was watching from my fissure, this is what I remembered. A light came from a large tent
in the cemetery square; it was illuminated like a world apart.
They're preparing a spectacle, I said. Some figures came and
went from the tent. I heard musicians playing and shouts. I
would have liked to hear, but I made out only distant echoes,
whistles, laughter, and the repeated strains of a fife. In the cold,
dark night, many people hurried to and fro. The cemetery was
aquiver, almost euphoric, and if it weren't deep into Lent there
might be still greater merrymaking.

The old procuress had to be there, too, because several times I
heard her strident laugh. She had a sharp, interminable laugh.
Then someone glided along the arcades in front of my cell,
walking soundless as a shadow. Then he started to run straight
toward the tent. I didn't see anything for a while because it
wasn't easy to make things out in the dark. Under the arcades
the torches were almost burnt out, while those in the tent still
shone brightly. When the people began to go away you could

hear the voices more clearly; happy people were rushing out of that world of warm light.

It was very cold and late. I kept watching, because all that activity, those sounds and voices, bewildered me. I think I'd forgotten how much confusion so many bodies in one place can create.

Looking out every once in a while is my way of reminding myself that I'm still here, alive, and part of this cemetery.

I admit, I watched then, yes. I covered my head with my tunic and stayed at my cell window. I couldn't say why I covered myself, since no one could see me in the dark. Yet this small rectangle of cold air always seemed like an eye that looks at me from outside my cell.

It had to be very late. The sacristan had closed the gate, and I heard him busying himself with his mass of keys. From here, I can make out only part of the cemetery, a part of the Arcade de la Vierge and one of the Lingères' arcades with their ossuaries, but I knew this place so well that the parts I can't see I reconstruct from memory.

The big tent emptied noisily. How could it hold so many people! Then, I saw a figure silhouetted against the torchlight and he was striking a man who was among the last to come out of the darkening tent. There was a cry. Was it because of this that the old crone laughed? The rapacious life always on the ready. And it was at that very moment that the spider web came to mind. In the glare of the torch the canvas was dark. All those tensed threads, the anticipation, the thump, the trajectory of a gesture. In that quick movement there was something well thought out.

Only at sunrise did I understand who had died. I saw a young man, followed by some beggars, lift your body onto the young man's shoulders. So, my friend, it's finished, I thought. But you shouldn't worry. They can't kill you. They set a trap for you, but you aren't an animal. They cannot mute your words simply by assassinating you! Your verses live in the air. Whoever comes here will scan them in his sleep, will hear them in dreams. You will sculpt them in their consciousness from afar, in death, in absence. It seems that the tactic of the spider web won, but in the long run we will win. The opposite tactic that affirms life will win.

I thought of these and other things. I watched closely. Covered with my tunic I watched that young man carry your body. It must have been very heavy. At a certain point the young man bent, stopped, and then went on, helped by someone. The two disappeared behind the wall. I couldn't see them any more from my crevice, so I don't know in which of the ditches you were buried. Certainly, "burying you" is only a manner of speaking, because someone like you is never buried. Truly, you endure. Maybe you are hiding yourself.

I continued to watch for a little while, before I retired. Thinking about these events brings up a cluster of feelings on which I then tried to reason. I saw you becoming every sound of your verses. People will make a dance of them; they'll make thoughts of them. Mothers will make chants with them. Every vowel will be a call to arms. Your body will not dry up and become hard as a tibia; it will go on as living matter. As seeds. Birds that migrate with the wind. Your rough common style was a noble language. I listened well to it, heard it come from the arcades in spreading fragments—your verses sung in late evening, and the laughter with the Sunday verses on visitors' day.

They made a snare for you, but they didn't realize that your astute laugh had already plowed this putrid soil. Yesterday morning when the sacristan brought me water he told me about some indecent, miserable rogues who'd been fighting for a week, and he told me that that faithless, bastard Turk got the lesson he deserved for his brazen verses in vulgar language. Then I felt unwell. I told him to take back his water and bread and that I didn't want to eat.

Today, before dawn, there was a lot of noisy rushing about, whistles, and hammer blows. I said to myself that the spectacle must be starting. And that in fact was what was happening, something I certainly hadn't seen before. I waited for the sunrise, staying at my small window for a moment, and then pulled back. I thought that without a doubt the curious as always would come and try to see me. I heard a loud commotion; after mid-day there were other sounds, music and trumpet peals. The bells had rung in full force many times. Then I heard voices declaiming, distant voices, alternating with the cries and litanies of the beggars excited by such a large audience. At a certain point I head furious galloping, and thudding hooves. It seemed as though everyone was dancing.

I lived through this enormous confusion with a feeling of peace, secure in my cell. It confirmed for me that I wouldn't have easily suffered the world, unless—if I hadn't been forced to be a novice—I had rebelled in some unforeseen way. Who knows how I would have used the irreversible course of my life. When I was young, I would have stayed a solitary woman or I would have departed on a long journey. What alternative does a different kind of person have? Agnes robed, ogled by employers, and burned at the stake by Inquisitors. Alix confined in a house? I don't know.

The whole day I kept praying and thinking. In a certain sense, I participated from a distance for I, too, am a citizen of this soil like the others. I, too, belong to that strange turmoil that possessed them. One might say that for a week the dead and the living have been contending with this putrid soil, with the entire world. I too was caught up in this convulsion.

Because a peculiar thing happened today.

A young man came at dawn, at a quiet moment while mass was being said and the crowd was gathered in a different part of the church. He stood beneath my cell. Since the cell's fissure is high and the earth under my cell is raised, no one can look inside from there; in order to look down, I would have to stretch up a little. So, I didn't see him. When the sacristan comes he always brings a stool on which he stands to give me my bread or to take the empty pitcher away. When the Turk brought me the May garland, he stood on tip-toe on something raised, like a stone, I think, because I heard him make an effort. I heard his puff and then a light noise, like a leap, and I didn't know if he mightn't have fallen to the ground with easy grace, he who was large and crippled. He neither tarried nor looked in my cell.

The fact is that if a person doesn't raise himself up from the ground, and if there are other noises—singing or shouting—I don't hear very well what anyone says, unless in the quiet of a summer afternoon the words are pronounced distinctly.

What would I have been able to say to that young man? Yes,

certainly, I heard him talk, but I barely understood some sentences here and there. Yet I listened carefully, straining to hear. I really wanted to understand.

But who has ever come to talk to me? I asked myself—to talk to me, to call me by name, a forgotten name, the irrelevant name of a remote shadow. The name of a vanished Heloise.

He said, "Alix, answer!" Answer, but answer what? How can I tell him where Alix is, I said to myself. She's a ghost who can appear, perhaps, among the people, but she's no longer who I am."

The young man kept asking. He recounted the events of his life. I grasped some phrases every once in a while and I made an effort to hear, but at times he spoke so softly that I was unable to hear anything. Only a lament. And then he insistently began to speak again. He talked to me; he wanted a sign, a word, only a small sign.

But a sign of what?

Apparently that young man had to make an important decision. But how could I help him, I who knew nothing of him? To advise him I would have had to discuss, reason, reflect—everything I can no longer do, not even for myself. Only occasionally, as in this week of turmoil, does an interior dialogue wash over me like a tide, pulling me into thoughts and remembrances. It breaks in, tears my silence, and then forsakes me again to my tranquil meditation.

So, I didn't answer.

I stayed leaning against the wall. The young man lingered for a long while; I think he sat down on the ground. I seemed to feel his presence through the thick wall.

He waited a long time, yes, and left around noon. Then something unusual happened to me. For a second, I felt a sudden stillness in my whole body. For a brief but intense moment, I felt distressed by an unidentifiable nostalgia. I felt that that young man was so like what I once was, or, rather, what I might perhaps have been. But if I understood well, a young man like him can go far. This century is his.

So, I would have said to him: Whatever you decide to do, it will be all right, if you . . . . No! I interrupted myself. What are you saying? What could you ever say to him? You would only have digressed, that's what. Who am I to advise him on what he must or mustn't do, on how he must or mustn't act. If I'd done that, I would really have taken myself for the Lady that he wanted to find so palpably before him.

Calling me Alix, he cast an eye on the real existence of a young woman from a distant past. But who can have given him my name? He truly grasped my life. For a moment he saw me—I, someone who had resembled him. However, despite everything, it's a recurrent illusion; something else: his obsessions, his elation. I asked myself, could he be a young Occitan from Provence, someone who carries the Provençal summer inside himself? Stuck in this dying land, he has coalesced mirages into an image, mirages in which no one any longer believes, mirages wasted on the stony roads of the South. I kept asking myself what this young man was doing here. I stayed thus, thinking in silence, and then I pulled back.

Shortly, absorbed in my thoughts, I heard the sacristan's shuffling walk. In the confusion of the day, he'd forgotten to bring me something to drink. I'd gone two days without water.

I heard him put down the stool, say something about the day's tiring work and his exhaustion. Then I saw the little terracotta pitcher placed in the hollow of my window. My throat was dry, but my body seemed light and suspended. For a week I hadn't felt like this, awake in the blaze of the presence, near and far, growing and present.

The sacristan kept talking. "Heavenly Saints," he said, "what a day! More than a Mystery, more than a confrontation, it was a battle. They destroyed everything. The bushes are trampled down and the tombs desecrated. A lost battle, a madness."

At that moment the young man from the morning returned. I heard his voice addressing the sacristan, "Sexton, Sir, I am a God-fearing man. I'm parched. May I drink from that pitcher up there?"

The sacristan was taken by surprise, or maybe he was too tired to react promptly. Anyway, he remained absolutely speechless for a long time, and then he started to shout. In the meantime, in that long suspended moment of surprise, the young man jumped on the stool and I clearly saw his hand take the pitcher. But he didn't drink. No! Totally infuriating the sacristan, he poured the water on himself, baptizing himself with the water. At least this is what I grasped from the sounds and curses that the sacristan repeated in a strident voice, "Vile shameless rascal! And why not baptize your feet, too? Why not your guts? That water, the recluse's water, by the holy saints— pouring it on yourself!"

Cursing, the sacristan rushed off, threatening to return with the guard. "May Saint Antoine burn you," he shouted, as he disappeared in the direction of the church. He was carrying the broken pitcher with him, I believe, because after a little while he brought me back a full one. I drank his water in great thirst. It was cool, almost sweet, I would say solid, and in the late evening I made my happy ablutions, because the scene had made me laugh.

Yes, and why not? Must a recluse always cry? With that act I recognized something joyous that I still feel now, late at night.

And then something even more extraordinary and unexpected happened. While the sacristan went muttering on his way, the young man jumped onto the stool and called to me, "Friend, know that I'm leaving for a long trip, but that I carry you with me as a perfect presence!"

I stayed where I was, surprised, with my face pressed against the wall, but I knew that he would not try to look inside the dark cell.

Perfect presence? How could he say that? My reclusion was an absolute choice for me, who had rejected an entire century; but for him who was hasting far away, what could it mean?

At that instant I heard some words, an echo, a distant peal, words that came from my body and I shouted out toward the tiny window, "The awakening of consciousness!" Just like that. And I felt everything coming together. Everything was clear.

The young man jumped down, then climbed back up on the stool, laughed, shouted. The whole cell was aclamor. I too laughed, seized by—how to say it—a blessed euphoria. My madness. The great gesture of my life. A brief second. His madness. The unnamable Thing to which I clung, and the Absolute. His mirage.

Then he called to me, "It's true, my God, how pitiful, taking myself so seriously! You're right, what you said is right! It's the soul that blooms and quickens, the soul that forbears and abides, that resists our bodies, which are so like catapults, horses, and walled cells. It's true. The beloved and the lover are but a single dream. Yes, Alix. But, Christ, what a dream, what a great dream we inhabit."

And then he left me.

CITY LIGHTS PUBLICATIONS